THE KRINAR CODE

A KRINAR WORLD NOVEL

EMMA CASTLE

Laura writing as Emma Castle

EMMA CASTLE
Dark and Edgy Romance

To Rich and Rhea,
Who showed me how life was meant to be, full of compassion and understanding. And for teaching me what it meant to be the original "Queenie."

1

———

"Ow!" Harper King swallowed a curse as she sucked on her pinched thumb. The big Corvette suspended above her was in decent shape, but the axle was dented all to hell. The owner had been pissed when she'd recommended he replace the axle or sell the car. Given that it was an expensive classic, he'd opted for the replacement, but he'd grumbled the entire time. Between the parts and labor to fix them, new axles could cost almost as much as the car itself. She didn't mind the work, but the customers at King Auto Repair usually didn't like the price.

"You okay, Harper?" A deep voice came from nearby. She glanced around and saw her older brother's boots as he stopped next to the car she was beneath.

"Yeah, I'm fine, Mason." She lay flat on her creeper

and pushed herself so she rolled out from underneath the Corvette. Her thumb still stung from where it had gotten caught in part of the undercarriage. She glowered at the car. "This axle, though, is going to have a very bad day tomorrow." She tilted her left wrist to check her watch. It was a little after nine at night, and her brother should have been working, not here in the garage.

Mason held out a hand, his brown eyes full of worry. He and Liam didn't approve of her running the mechanic shop on her own, but she was damned good at it, and they needed to get with the century.

Mason's eyes darkened with shadows, and his voice lowered. "Liam and I have a meeting tonight. You got any more jobs, or can you watch the bar with Neil for the rest of the night?"

She let Mason lift her up onto her feet, and she glanced around at the shop. "Yeah, I can watch it for you." She didn't mind tending bar most of the time, but her true love was the auto shop.

King Auto Repair shared a building with King's Bar, the bar that her brothers ran together. It wasn't much, but given that Lawrence, Kansas, was a little college town of just under a hundred thousand people, it passed for the center of the local nightlife.

Harper wiped at the sweat on her brow. It was quiet. The usual sounds of electric drills, men whistling, car hoods slamming, and the symphony of choking engines, sputtering motors, and hydraulic ramps going up and down were absent since they'd closed two hours ago. Her two employees, Jeff and Alan, had already left for the day. The shop had closed at seven, and she'd been so deep into her work that she'd lost track of time. It wasn't the first time that had happened. When she was working, she could dive so deep into the job that the rest of the world just fell away.

"You and Liam will be careful, won't you?" she asked him.

Mason, at twenty-nine, and Liam, at thirty-one, were grown men, but Harper still worried about them. Ever since they had lost their parents on K-Day, the day the Krinar invaded Earth, the three of them seemed to be standing alone against the world.

"We'll be fine," Mason promised her. He and Liam wouldn't let her join their meetings because they thought it was too dangerous for her. They were running a resistance group out of the back of the bar. Every couple of weeks they held a meeting with local men and women who wanted to find a way to resist the Krinar occupation. But even if they had let her join, she wouldn't have. Humans couldn't fight the Krinar— or the Ks, as most humans called them—and it was just out of plain old human stubbornness that they even tried.

From the moment they had arrived five years ago,

the aliens had taken charge, almost effortlessly. They looked human enough, just insanely attractive, like muscled supermodels. They weren't skinny and gray with black oval eyes like many people obsessed with extraterrestrials had expected them to be, and they sure as shit didn't need help phoning home like E.T. The Krinar were stronger, faster, and smarter than humans. They lived for thousands of years and had technology that made Earth science look like humans were still banging rocks together trying to make fire.

We never stood a chance when they invaded. What makes anyone think we have one now?

Harper sighed and rubbed her grease-covered hands on a towel and watched Mason walk back through the hall that connected the bar to the garage. Then she busied herself with closing down the shop. She made a note in her calendar to call the Corvette owner tomorrow with an update, but the simple task of writing tended to make her head hurt.

She'd been diagnosed with severe dyslexia in high school. She'd graduated high school, barely, but she hadn't been able to get into college. Numbers were easier to write, but words and names? It was like she was watching the letters dance around the page, and it gave her a migraine. If her father hadn't discovered she had a knack for mechanics, she didn't know where she might have ended up.

Thankfully, engines, mechanics, and electronics all

came to her with stunning clarity. When she'd turned eighteen, she'd been able to take over her father's repair shop.

Harper paused to look at the photo of her parents that hung behind the reception desk inside the shop. In the photo her parents were standing outside the repair shop entrance. It had been taken nearly twenty years ago when she was only four. Her father beamed with pride, and her mother was looking at him with admiration. They'd been so in love, so in tune with one another.

And they were gone.

A deep sting lanced through Harper's chest, a pain of loss and sorrow that would never fully heal, no matter how much time had passed. No one deserved to die the way they had.

She kissed the tips of her fingers and pressed them to the glass of the framed photo. "Night, Mom and Dad."

Then she lowered the shop doors, set the alarm system, turned off the lights, and passed through the hall and into the small office between the auto shop and the bar. The large desk against the far wall by the single window was littered with paperwork from both the shop and the bar. Harper growled. Every night she came back here she had to clean up after Mason and Liam. They were great at dealing with vendors and customers, but they sucked at basic business organization and bookkeeping. She practically had to pester them to keep up their records.

Harper shoved the papers aside to retrieve the folded set of clean clothes she brought to work every day. Shop work always left her khaki work suit covered in grease. She changed into her jean shorts and T-shirt with the King's Bar logo, a retro-looking crown beneath the King name in a bold stylistic font. Then she removed her work boots and slipped on some simple leather sandals. She wasn't girly, not compared to most girls she knew, but after work she did like to feel a bit more feminine, even if she was tending bar for her older brothers.

As she exited the office, she could hear the rowdy sounds of the bar over the thrumming bass of the bar's modern jukebox. She opened the door and scanned the room. The walnut wood tables and even the bar itself were full, which was typical for a Saturday night. The kids from the University of Kansas loved to come and hang out after tough classes all week.

"Harper!" Jessie Lang, one of the full-time waitresses, grinned and waved at Harper. Jessie carried a full tray of beers toward a table of men who were watching the nearest flat-screen TV hanging from one of the bar's support beams. They whooped as someone made a touchdown. College football was serious business in Kansas, and any good bar worth its salt would have a dozen TVs up and running with the latest games on.

Harper smiled and waved at Jessie as they shared an amused shrug at the men talking football stats. She and Jessie were close in age, and she usually spent her free weekends hanging out with Jessie.

A lot had changed since the Krinar had arrived. They had shut down production of beef and poultry, for one thing. Enforced veganism, most people called it, and she had to admit, of all the jackbooted declarations she had expected to come down the pipe from their new overlords, that was pretty damn close to the bottom of the list.

But it had hit the Midwest hard. Many cities became ghost towns, and people had moved away and sold their grazing fields, which were unsuitable for crops and were now empty and valueless. It was why so much resistance had formed here against the Krinar. Mason and Liam had mobilized their friends who'd lost work when their homes had been sucked into the economic black hole the Krinar invasion had created. And their friends had brought other friends, and so on.

All because those damn aliens didn't eat meat.

If I ever meet one of them, I'll shove a cheeseburger right down their throat. The rebellious thought made her smile widen. Having to eat the plant-based protein burger patties made her gag.

7

"How's it going?" she asked her friend as she joined her at the bar.

Jessie laughed, her dark-brown eyes bright with her natural joy. "Busy as hell, and Katie's got the flu. You mind taking orders from those tables in the corner?" Jessie reached across the bar, where she placed a new drinks order ticket for their bartender, Neil, who was busy mixing.

"Sure." Harper gave Neil a nod, and he flexed his tattooed arms as he shook the martini mixer. The wall behind him was covered with a hundred bottles of decent liquor, as well as some more expensive scotch and brandy. People came from miles around to King's Bar—students, farmers, blue-collar workers, and even some upper-middle-class folk. Her parents had left a legacy of openness and welcoming to all. Harper could gripe about a lot of things with regard to her older brothers, but they were great at keeping the bar fun, except on nights they hosted resistance meetings in the back storeroom. Those always made her nervous.

Harper bit her lip and glanced toward the *Employees Only* sign hanging on the door. The closely spaced letters jumbled about and made her grimace. She'd tried to develop her own shorthand to work with Neil when giving him orders, but it still was a challenge.

"Sure, Jessie. I'll cover the two tables in the back corner." She picked up a pen and notepad from the bar, her stomach cramping at the thought of having to write down drink orders.

She reached the first table, where a tall man lounged back in his chair, watching the room. His blue eyes swept to her face as she approached, and Harper's heart jolted as she felt the full focus of his stormy blue gaze. Damn, the man was fine. *More* than fine. He had long legs and narrow hips, but he also had those broad shoulders all women loved. His red plaid shirt hung open to reveal a gray T-shirt underneath that clung a little too snug to his skin, which hinted at a hard chest and chiseled abs.

Wow. Where had this hunk of man meat come from? Harper blushed and stared at her sandals. It was not okay to objectify a guy, right? She was a total feminist—she had to be around her overprotective brothers. But damn if this guy didn't make her want to wolf-whistle.

Harper finally looked at the man before her again, and that was a mistake. "W-what can I get you?"

His golden-blond hair fell into his eyes, and he casually brushed it back. How could such a simple gesture make her knees buckle? The sleeves of his shirt were rolled up to his elbows, exposing the muscles of his forearms. Harper swallowed hard. Damn again— she was having a serious attraction to this complete stranger. Something that was totally not like her. She usually kept to herself these days. She'd dated a lot in the past, sure, but lately she'd been so focused on work she'd lost track.

"I'll take an India Pale Ale. Whatever kind you recommend. Thanks." His lips curved in a telltale bad-boy smile that scared her shitless. It was a smile that promised nothing but broken hearts. An IPA, that was easy enough to remember. She lowered her notepad in relief, not bothering to write that order down. She started to head back to the bar to grab his drink, but as she passed by the next table, a man grabbed her arm.

"Not so fast, sweetheart. We need drinks too. We've been here ten minutes already."

Harper gritted her teeth. She didn't mind being called *sweetheart* by a boyfriend, but by some tool like this? She eyed the rough-looking man, and his friends all snickered at her open discomfort. She wanted to flip them off, but that wasn't going to help. She plastered on a reluctant smile and lifted her pad up.

"What can I get you?" *And by that I mean, "What can I have Neil spit in?"*

The men all started throwing exotic drink orders at her, and she struggled, frantically penning down their orders, but within seconds the panic set in. Her pen froze, and she closed her eyes briefly.

"What's the matter with you? Why aren't you writing our orders down?" the first asshole demanded.

"I am!" she snapped. "I just need a minute. I" She turned again to list the drinks, but she couldn't correctly spell some of the more complicated orders, and then it was too late. The letters began to almost quiver on the page, and she suddenly couldn't decipher her own writing.

"You stupid or something?" one of the men asked her. His companions broke out into more laughter.

Harper grabbed the nearest water glass and threw its contents into the face of the man who'd called her stupid. He surged to his feet and backhanded her so fast she never saw the blow coming.

Pain ripped through her and she stumbled back, clutching her face in shock. A hush settled over the crowd, and Harper shot a glare at the man. She wasn't afraid to throw a punch, but she was outnumbered. And with her luck, she'd break her hand on his jaw.

"You have a problem?" the man who'd struck her now snapped at her.

"Out! I want you and your asshole buddies out of here!" Harper yelled. While this wasn't technically her bar, she felt like a part owner of it, the same way her brothers felt about her garage. And like the sign over the bar said, "*We reserve the right to refuse service to anyone who's an asshole.*"

"Oh yeah?" The man spread his arms out wide, noting the lack of security coming to restrain him. Normally Neil would have been right there, kicking this guy's ass, but he'd broken his leg last week on his motorcycle and was stuck on crutches behind the bar. "Who's gonna make me?"

"Pardon me," a deep masculine voice said right behind her as two large hands settled on her waist. She was lifted up and set aside by the gorgeous blond Adonis from the other table.

"I believe the lady asked you to leave. And your asshole buddies."

The asshole and his friends all stood. Six to one—those weren't good odds. "Is that so?"

"That's so."

"Hey, you really don't need to" Harper touched the Adonis's rock-hard shoulder.

The Adonis swung a fist fast, almost too fast to see. It connected with the asshole's jaw, and he stumbled back, knocking over three chairs, and his head collided with the wall in a heavy *thunk*. He didn't stir. One of his friends knelt down to check his pulse.

"Chase is out cold," the other man said. They all turned to face the Adonis again.

"I suggest you get out. Now. And take your trash with you," Adonis growled in a tone that sent shivers of dread through Harper. She'd seen plenty of men try to fake being a badass over the years, but this guy wasn't faking. He was dangerous. *Really* dangerous. And he'd just saved her ass.

The group of jerks rushed out of the bar, only two of them stopping to lift Chase up and carry him out.

Neil followed them to the door on his crutches, scowling the entire way. Adonis watched them go, his arms crossed. Once they were gone, the conversations in the bar went back to normal, and the stares of curious bargoers eventually drifted away from them.

"Are you all right?" The man cupped her chin as he tilted her face toward his, checking where she'd been struck. A flare of warmth seeped from his palm into her skin, and she tried not to shiver at the feminine awareness of him that made her shyly try to step away.

"He got me pretty good, but I'll be okay." She needed to escape the heat of his gentle touch. The man was gorgeous, but in a purely masculine way. A blush spread over her face, and her right cheek throbbed hotly with the added rush of blood.

"You'll need to ice your cheek, or it's going to swell and bruise. Come." He caught her hand and started pulling her along behind him toward the bar. Too stunned to object, she followed along.

"Oh my God, Harper!" Jessie met them at the bar, along with Neil. "Should I get Mason and Liam?"

Jessie's gaze darted to Adonis, and she choked down whatever else she might have said next. She just blinked in a dazed way that Harper completely understood. This man was just the kind of perfect male specimen that would leave any girl gobsmacked.

"I'm okay, Jessie. Mr....er...what's your name?" Harper asked.

"Seth Jackson. Call me Seth." His stormy blue eyes were still filled with concern.

"Thank you, Seth. Why don't you go back to your table, and I'll get your...IPA, wasn't it? On the house."

"Thank you. But first I want to make sure you are all right." His lips slid into a slow smile that only intensified her blush. Seth looked toward Jessie. "Can you get me some ice, please?"

"Yeah, sure, hang on." Jessie retrieved the ice and a towel and handed them to Seth.

"Sit," he ordered. Harper found herself gently but firmly planted on a barstool. He wrapped the bagged ice in the towel and put it to her bruised cheek. She reached up, expecting him to let her take over, but their hands touched when she tried to hold the ice up. An electric pulse jumped between them, and her body seemed to hum inside from the connection.

Wow. She was turned on just being close to him. The ice had already started to soak the towel and drip down her arm and his. She was captivated by him and the way his gaze seemed to swallow her up, leaving her mind free of thoughts and instead focused only on sensations.

"Thanks. I think I've got it now," she managed to say, embarrassed by how breathless she sounded.

"Okay, but I'm going to stay here and keep an eye on you. You might have a concussion." He held out his hand. "Let me take your pad. I can get orders for you."

"No!" she almost yelped. She did not want him to see her hastily scribbled and disjointed words. "I mean, thanks, but I'll be fine."

"Harper, he's right, I shouldn't have asked you to take orders. Not with your"

"Jessie!" She cut her friend off. She didn't like people knowing about her dyslexia. It was a common enough condition, but there were always people who didn't understand and who gave her funny looks or treated her differently when they found out. She did not want Seth to look at her like that.

Because I'm not broken, dammit.

She had to remind herself of that. Having severe dyslexia did not mean that she was damaged or not smart. Quite the opposite. People with dyslexia actually absorbed too much information at once, and while that made reading difficult, it did enhance her awareness of more details than the average person, especially visually. It made her one heck of a mechanic. She could rebuild practically anything mechanical from scratch, all by instinct.

"Seriously, go, I'm fine. I'll bring you your drink in a moment." She tried to wave him off, but Seth just grinned.

"You're bossy, but cute as a button. I'm not going anywhere, and neither are you. Keep your butt in that chair." He held out a hand to Jessie. "Give me a pad and tell me which tables need orders."

Jessie gave Harper an apologetic look as she gave a spare pad and pen to Seth.

"Just three tables near the door. We should be good unless someone waves you over."

"Got it." Seth headed over to a table, his back to Harper as he talked to the men and women there.

"Damn, that ass is tight enough to bounce a quarter off of." Jessie giggled and nudged Harper, who was staring at it too. He filled out those blue jeans nicely.

"You need to hit that tonight," Jessie said as she loaded a tray with a couple of margaritas.

Harper rolled her eyes and adjusted the bag of ice against her cheek. Her fingers were a little chilly but not frozen.

"I'm not tapping anything," she muttered. "Not tonight, anyway."

"Pity. He looks like he wants to eat you up...or eat you out." Jessie was giggling again.

"Get your mind out of the gutter."

"Girl, it never left." Jessie's brown eyes twinkled before she trotted off to deliver the margaritas to a waiting table.

Harper watched Seth take more orders, and she sighed. God, she would love to sleep with a guy like that, but she was done with the whole dating-sexy-guys thing. It didn't end well. Her last boyfriend, Xander, had been too cute for his own good, and he knew it.

Eventually his hands had wandered off, and the rest of him had followed. Harper had gone home to their shared apartment the night of their one-year anniversary and spent two hours baking and cooking for their dinner. By ten p.m. she'd finally blown out the candles, removed her black high heels and her sexy little red dress, and put the food in the fridge. It had been obvious he'd forgotten and wasn't coming.

She'd crawled into bed and cried so much she'd smeared mascara all over her pillowcase. The next morning, she'd called him and he'd apologized, and then she'd heard the other woman's voice in the background asking who it was.

She'd never trusted any good-looking man after that, and if she was being truly honest, she didn't trust *any* man fully after that. It wasn't in her nature to leave herself so vulnerable, but Xander had made her want to trust him, and their chemistry had been so good that she'd let her hormones make all the decisions.

Still, she wasn't opposed to dating or even casual sex with nice, normal guys. But a man like Seth? No. He was trouble. She was done with guys like him for sure. They were too easy to fall for, and she was done with being a sucker for a good-looking guy. Seth was trouble, and she was going to stay the hell away from him.

2

T he mission was in jeopardy.

Sef was supposed to be keeping a low profile, posing as "Seth," a human male ready to join the resistance that the King brothers, Mason and Liam, were running out of the back of the bar. Instead, he was taking drink orders after having almost killed a human who'd struck their sister, Harper, the curvy little human with sweet eyes and a scent that made him want to growl with longing. He was lucky he had pulled his punch; otherwise, he would've crushed the man's jaw and possibly killed the bastard. Though he probably deserved it, that would have created even more complications for the mission.

Focus on being calm. She's okay. The idiots are gone. She's safe.

If there was one thing he hated, it was violence

toward a female. From the moment Harper King had walked up to his table, he'd caught her sweet feminine scent untarnished by heavy perfumes and had gotten hard fast. She was definitely his type. Small, curvy, and feisty. But she was off-limits.

Normally when he saw a female he wanted, he would seduce her, with her willing cooperation, and then fuck her for a week straight until he'd gotten her out of his system. But if he did that with Harper, it risked his ability to earn the trust of her brothers. For now he would have to play the gentleman, to use a phrase he'd picked up recently. But damned if the little female didn't tempt him almost beyond reason and control.

As a Krinar male, he could claim her as a charl, which was the Krinar term for a human companion, but he had never taken a charl. It was too lasting, too intimate of a relationship. He was eight thousand years old, and while he'd had hundreds of lovers over the years, he had never chosen to be a cheren to any of them. He wasn't so foolish and impulsive as his twin brother, Soren. Taking a charl would be permanent. Any human taken as a charl would be given nanocytes, which would extend their lives indefinitely at peak age and peak condition, keeping them forever young. Sef had never considered any female he'd met to be someone he would share forever with, but Harper

King was making his mind and desires stray into dangerous territory.

How had this human so suddenly captivated him? Perhaps he was getting soft spending so much time on Earth. Or maybe it was the fact that Soren had recently taken a human charl, and through their shared bond he was sensing such feelings of contentment that it made him long for a charl of his own.

If that was the case, he was going to punch his brother the next time he saw him. Such feelings of desire, sentimentality, and intimacy were harmful to his mission.

He zoned out, writing down drink orders and waiting patiently for the humans to finish ordering. Then he walked back to the bar and slipped the bartender the order.

"Thanks, man. We appreciate the help tonight. I'm Neil." The bartender held out his hand over the polished walnut counter.

Sef slapped his palm into the other man's. He seemed strong, for a human. "Seth Jackson. Happy to help."

"Thanks for saving the kid. Harper's sweet. If I'd been closer and not dragged down with these damn crutches, I would've done exactly what you did and thrown out that trash."

Sef nodded and smiled, but a flicker of a strange emotion shot through him as Neil called Harper sweet.

For one split second he imagined punching Neil and breaking his jaw.

Was he jealous? Over a human female? If Soren ever found out, he would never live it down. Soren was the Krinar ambassador to Earth, and he had recently done a very human thing and gotten engaged to the American president's daughter, Bianca Wells.

Sef glimpsed his reflection in the glass behind the bar and for a second didn't recognize himself. Despite the fact that Sef had left for this mission a few days ago, he still hadn't gotten used to how his looks had changed for this mission. Like all Krinar, he had brown eyes and brown hair, though his was a little more russet, a color unique to his family and their region of their planet, Krina. But for this mission he had been given contact lenses and a hair treatment to turn his hair a golden blond.

Humans wouldn't suspect him to be Krinar so long as he kept his super-strength and increased speed hidden from them. That was why striking that bastard who'd hit Harper tonight had been so dangerous. Sef had almost blown his cover just by punching him. But after seeing Harper hit, he'd nearly lost his mind.

There was something about her that called to him and played upon his protective instincts. He didn't like the way just looking at her made his blood hum and his body ache for dark pleasures. Already he wanted to sink his teeth into her neck and taste her blood. The high it would give them both would be unbelievable. But he had to hold back. He needed to stay undercover, and the last thing he needed was to perpetuate the rumors that Ks were blood drinkers. They were, of course, but his people wished to keep that quiet for now.

Sef spent the next two hours helping Jessie and Neil manage the bar before it was finally closing time. Harper's face was still a nasty shade of red, and he examined it while Neil cleaned the bar and Jessie tidied up the tables.

"I'm fine." She blushed and tried to push his hand away. He didn't like it when she pulled away from him, but given his height and build, it was understandable that a small female like Harper would be wary of him at first. He had no such problems with Krinar females, but at that moment only one female mattered, and she was human.

"Honey, you aren't fine. That asshole landed one hell of a blow." In order to soothe her, Sef slipped into the more casual words and phrases he'd learned. It was one of the many talents that made him such a good guardian for undercover operations.

Harper winced. "If he hadn't had all his friends with him, I would've taken him out." The conviction of her statement confused him.

"You would *date* that man?"

Now Harper was confused. "No, *take out*. Beat to a pulp. Taken out on a stretcher."

Sef chuckled. "Oh, of course. Adorable and blood-thirsty. Are you trying to drive me crazy?" he muttered.

"Huh?" Harper blinked and stared at him.

"Hey, Seth?" Neil called out. "Come meet the bosses." Neil nodded at the *Employees Only* door. Two tall human males, almost as tall as him, came out through the door as it swung open. They looked similar to Harper, but where she was small and feminine, they were tall and masculine, decent specimens of human males. Krinar females would be attracted to these two if they ever visited an X-club or a Krinar Center.

"Mason, Liam," Neil called out, and pointed at Sef with his thumb. "This guy saved little Harper's ass a while ago."

"I didn't need saving." Harper's adorable grumble went unheard by all but him. The Krinar had heightened senses, including hearing.

"What happened?" Liam asked. He and Mason came over to Harper by the edge of the bar.

"Some asshole slapped me," Harper admitted, shame coloring her tone. "Caught me off guard."

Neil finished the story. "Seth here knocked him out cold with one punch and sent his friends packing. They had to carry the guy out."

"Jesus, Harper, come get us next time." Mason tried to look at Harper's face, but she turned away, annoyed.

"Hey, thanks, man." Liam offered a hand. "Seth, was it?"

Sef took it, then shook Mason's as well. "Seth Jackson. You're welcome. No one hits a woman on my watch." *And I would have killed the bastard if there hadn't been any witnesses,* he added silently.

"What can we do to make it up to you?" Liam offered.

And this was what made his risky action tonight worthwhile. He had hoped to ingratiate himself to the King brothers somehow, and this was a perfect opportunity.

"Actually, I'm passing through, but I could use a job. Maybe a recommendation of where to stay? I'll be around a couple of months." He hoped the brothers would offer him a way to stay close until he could infiltrate their operation.

"He was pretty helpful tonight," Jessie volunteered. "We were down a waitress, and he was great."

"Oh?" Liam glanced at Neil and Harper, who both nodded in agreement. "Well...would you like that? We pay a few bucks above minimum wage, and any tips you make are entirely yours."

"Thanks. That would be great." Sef grinned and noticed Harper shoot him a glance. He wished he could read her thoughts. Her expressions were so guarded.

"We even have a spare room in the apartment next

door. Harper lives on the first floor. You could have the room on the second floor if you're interested. It needs some work, but we would only charge two hundred a month."

"Sounds like my lucky day. I can afford that." Sef could afford whatever he needed, but he was here to play the role of a human drifter, moving from town to town. The King brothers weren't idiots—it would take time to win their trust and convince them to let him join their movement.

"Harper, why don't you get him a bar T-shirt for work and show him the apartment. We can handle the paperwork tomorrow," Mason suggested.

Harper blew out a little breath but didn't argue. "This way." She led him to a door that connected to the auto shop. There was an office in the small space between the two businesses but it was separated by a door to give it privacy. Harper opened a large cardboard box beside the desk and shot a glance at him, sizing him up.

"XL, I assume?" she asked before turning back to the box.

"Yeah." He stared at her curvy ass as she bent over, and he licked his lips, unable to stop imagining how it would feel to bend her over the table and pound that soft little bottom, listening to her scream his name in pleasure.

No. Off-limits. Could blow everything.

She straightened and faced him, holding a King's Bar T-shirt. He took it and studied the crown logo.

"King's, huh? You need a shirt that says Queen's as well."

Harper's eyes brightened, and she suddenly smiled. "My dad used to call my mom Queenie. She loved that."

"Did something happen to them?" he asked.

He already knew they were dead. During the Great Panic that had followed the day his people had invaded, many humans had died. The chaos had been hard to prevent. Soren, his brother, had done much to quell fears and resistance early on by working with the human president here in the United States, but there was still violence, riots and deaths that had been unavoidable—and very one-sided. Even with the Coexistence Treaty in place, there were still anti-K groups and all the dangers that came with that.

"They died during the Great Panic. They were on a bridge in their car. Someone blew up the bridge, thinking it would hurt the Ks, but all it did was kill forty-three innocent people, all humans. They were trapped, drowned. They never even found my mother's body." Her voice roughened, and she wrapped her arms around herself, as though she needed a hug.

Sef hated to think that innocent humans had suffered because of them. His people didn't want to hurt anyone. They wanted to—*needed* to—live peacefully alongside them, but until humans learned to accept that their world had changed, his people had to retain control.

And it wasn't like they had been terribly good custodians before the Krinar had arrived. Between pollution and overpopulation, this world needed their protection in order to survive. Sef's people needed Earth because their own sun was dying. They had only a few thousand years to make Earth stable before they could bring the rest of the Krinar here. Which meant the humans needed to learn to share. And though they didn't know it yet, the humans owed their very existence to the Krinar.

"Thanks for the shirt," he said. "I'm sorry about your parents." He paused, holding his breath. "Do you hate them? The Ks, I mean?"

Harper's gaze shifted to a distant look, and her mouth hardened.

"*Hate* is such a strong word. I don't *hate* them. But I want them to leave. They've ruined so much, especially here. Middle America is dying. They want us to grow fruits and vegetables, but some people need meat protein in their diets, and not all farmlands have the right soil to be turned from grazing fields into crop-yielding land. Not to mention it's a bit off-putting being told what to do. Un-American, you might say."

Sef smirked at that. Stubbornness was a trait one could apply to this nation.

"Our way of life was taken away, and we didn't get any say in how to stay alive. It's one thing to have lofty ideals and to force people to bend to your will and all that, but if you don't stop to look at how it impacts others, doesn't that make *you* a monster? The Ks were wrong to do what they did. This is *our* home. We live, fight, and die on this little blue planet. The Ks could go somewhere else if they can't respect us and our lives here. They have the technology to travel anywhere— I've seen it."

"You have?" That surprised him. His files on the King family hadn't suggested she'd encountered any Krinar up close.

"I mean, not in person, but I've seen pictures and videos." Suddenly Harper's eyes were bright with excitement. "They're all close-lipped about what they can do, but FTL, or faster-than-light travel, is no small feat. Plus we know they have special healing devices, and..." She blushed again and cleared her throat. "Sorry, don't get me started talking about Krinar technology. But I'd give a small fortune to be able to take apart even one of their children's toys for ten minutes." She grabbed a set of keys hanging from a hook on the wall and left the office. Sef followed behind, and she led him through the darkened garage and out another door. He wanted to know more about what she thought about Krinar technology, but it was wise to keep his mouth shut.

"The apartment building connects to the far end of my shop."

"*Your* shop?" He'd assumed her brothers also owned the auto shop. He'd only glanced at her dossier before he'd come here. She wasn't his target, after all.

"Yep. Brothers got the bar; I got the garage. I'm good with machines, always have been. Dad let me take over after I graduated high school."

"No college?"

"No—self-taught. So what? Bill Gates never graduated either." He smelled a faint trace of panic in the air just as he had back in the bar when he'd asked her to give him her notepad. She'd refused. There was something there that bothered him, but he couldn't figure out what.

"So, there's another door outside you can get in if you want." She opened the door from the auto shop to a stairwell and held up a ring with a green fob. "This key with the green fob opens the outside door to the stairs, and the red fob opens your apartment. It's that one up there." She nodded up the stairs. He trailed behind her as she led him to the apartment.

The room was dark and musty as he searched for a light switch. There was a small kitchen, a bedroom, and a little living room. Adequate, if a bit small for his tastes.

"I'll grab some fresh bed linens. We keep the mattress bare until we rent the room." She went to the linen closet by the bedroom and pulled out some sheets. "I washed these a few days ago. The fridge is empty, but there's a supermarket just a block away. Only it's not open right now. Have you had dinner?"

Sef shook his head. He wasn't terribly hungry, but if she was offering to cook, he'd be more than happy to accept—to protect his cover, of course.

"Why don't you get settled and come down to my apartment when you're done. I'll whip something up. I always end up having a late dinner on nights like these."

He watched her walk away, unable to deny the sway of her bottom in those jean shorts. When she shut the door behind her, he gave his head a little shake and focused on fixing up his bedding. He then removed a small device from his pocket and sent an encrypted message to Arus, one of his friends, who was also a powerful and influential Krinar. Arus was the one who'd given him this mission.

Sef: *I've made contact with the King brothers and have a job at their bar as well as living accommodations nearby. My next goal is to gain their trust and show sympathy toward the resistance.*

A few seconds later, Arus responded.

Arus: *Excellent. We will send a fabricator and jansha healing device now that you have secured lodging. We will send you items to set up localized surveillance of the King properties.*

He sent Arus a thank-you reply and then locked the communication device inside one of the air vents near the front door. Humans tended to look under mattresses and inside bathrooms for hidden items, but never in vents by the entrance. It felt too vulnerable, but that was what made it a perfect hiding spot. It would be only a matter of minutes before a small drone-like device flew here to his apartment to deliver his other requested technology.

He put the sheets and pillows on the bed and retrieved a couple of thick blankets from the closet. When he got into the bedroom he noticed the window was open and on his bed lay a parcel of small items. The drone had already come and gone in his absence of a mere thirty seconds. After he was done hiding the Krinar technology and laying the blankets on his bed, he went downstairs and knocked on Harper's door. Even though this was a bad idea, he couldn't deny the appeal of having the little Earth human all to himself in her living space. The subtle intimacy excited him. Maybe he could steal a kiss. One kiss from a human wouldn't put his mission in jeopardy, would it?

3

Why the hell am I so nervous?

Harper didn't want to analyze the answer to that question too closely. She opened her apartment door, and Seth stepped inside. She moved back, as he dwarfed her in the doorway. He had to be close to six foot seven. Her head didn't even come close to the top of his shoulders. She had to admit she liked that, *a lot.*

Seth faced her and inhaled deeply. "Smells good." For a second she thought he was smelling *her*, and a shiver of delight rippled through her despite herself.

Harper forgot all about the food as she took in the sight of his muscular body. His shoulders strained at the edges of his red plaid button-up shirt, yet he was perfectly proportioned with a trim waist, the kind of waist a woman wanted to wrap her legs around. But that was a dangerous thought. He moved deeper into her apartment with a panther's grace, and she didn't doubt his rough-and-tumble side after having watched him deck that asshole earlier tonight.

"I...thanks." Harper tried to remember that he was commenting on her food, and she rushed past him back toward the kitchen. She had grilled some chicken breasts on a skillet with oil, lemon, and rosemary and put together a basic salad. She wasn't a pro, but she had mastered a few recipes to keep her from hitting the fast-food joints too often.

"Chicken?" Seth leaned his elbows on the tall bar that formed part of her kitchen as he watched her.

"Yeah. I know the Ks shut down the chicken and beef production plants, but I know a guy. He has free-range chickens, cattle, and goats. He sells eggs and meat products and goat cheese to the local families. That's not illegal, so the Ks haven't shown up to stop him."

Seth's eyes glittered, and he chuckled. "A town of rebels? I like it."

Harper almost told him he was more right than he realized. She considered telling him about the local resistance, even though she wasn't a part of it. It was pointless fighting the Ks, causing unrest and more violence. It wasn't the answer. The Ks weren't evil—it wasn't like they were bent on destroying the world. But they hadn't been forthcoming with their motivations either. Harper wanted to believe that if the humans and the Krinar could just meet and really talk a few things out, it could go a long way. But the Krinar were so secretive. It was hard to trust a race of aliens who wouldn't talk to you and treated you like misbehaving children.

She focused on Seth again as she cut the chicken into strips and placed them on top of the salads. He was classically handsome, with a strong jaw and aquiline nose, but his lips were a little too full, making him look sensual rather than statuesque. They looked kissable and tempting. She didn't want to focus on his eyes because if she did, she would daydream about their deep, rich blue color. Right now they were almost a rich China blue, but earlier she had seen a darker, stormier color in them at the bar when he had defended her.

"So, Seth. Where are you from?" She kept her tone casual because he was watching her a little too keenly, like a man who was contemplating the risks and rewards of making a move on her. That would be trouble. There was nothing better and in some ways nothing worse than being the sole focus of a gorgeous man.

"I'm from everywhere. Military brat. Dad was in the army. Can't seem to shake the travel bug out of my system." He shot her a half-cocked smile, somewhere between a grin and a sexy smirk, something that always tore a woman between wanting to kiss a man or slap him.

Damn, this Seth guy was dangerous. She tugged at the neck of her T-shirt, feeling the telltale flush of arousal flare inside her. Why hadn't she changed into something more attractive?

No. Bad Harper. You can't sleep with him, so there's no reason to dress up.

"Army, huh? How about your mom?"

"She's an accountant. My dad's retired, but she still runs a small office. They live in Boulder now." Seth picked up the two salad bowls and took them to the already set kitchen table, his body lightly brushing against hers from behind. A flare of excitement and wild heat passed between them, and her breath hitched. "Come and sit," he said. "I bet you've been on your feet all day." He swept his eyes down her body, pausing on her feet still in her strappy sandals before he met her eyes. Harper sucked in a breath. She could've sworn his scorching gaze almost touched her in a tangible caress.

"Thanks. I am pretty beat," she admitted. "You want a beer or wine?" She started for the fridge again.

Strong hands caught her by the waist and steered her back toward the table.

Normally she would have hated it if a man tried to steer her around like that, but when Seth took control, somehow it was like he was caring for her, spoiling her.

What a strange and...wonderful thought. Maybe he wasn't like Xander after all.

"Allow me," Seth said, his eyelashes sliding down to half-mast in that purely male, bedroom way that sent her into a wild flash of arousal. She was sucked in by the seductive lure of his rich baritone voice.

Okay... This man seemed to have been created out of thin air from the fantasies of women around the world. That meant something about him had to be wrong. He had to be a womanizer or married or something. After all, what did they say about when something looked too good to be true?

The last thing she needed was to be in another relationship, but if she could have one night of fun with him, why not? There was something about him that promised long, sweaty nights and sweet, intimate mornings. Things she'd once longed for in a relationship and now feared. Because good-looking men couldn't be trusted not to stray, and she couldn't trust herself not to be the fool who got her heart broken again and again.

She sat down at the table and had the good fortune of watching him bend over a little to reach for a bottle of wine inside her fridge. Damn, those jeans fit his body just right. It made her thirsty just to look at him. He quickly found a bottle of shiraz and two glasses. He handed her one and sat down opposite her at the table.

"So, what are your plans if you're just passing through?"

"I'm hoping to work for a bit and then head to Colorado, maybe settle down."

Harper took a bite of her salad and watched him spear a piece of chicken on his fork and look at it in momentary concern before he ate it.

"Do you like it? Is it too dry?" She immediately felt like an idiot. She shouldn't care if he didn't like her cooking. She wasn't lacking in self-confidence, at least not in general terms.

"It's surprisingly good. I'm not usually a fan of grilled chicken, but this is fantastic." Her shoulders lowered as she released the tension in them.

"Relax, Harper. I'm not going to bite," he teased her.

She choked on a swallow of her wine. "What?"

He took another bite, watching her as he chewed and swallowed. "You look half-terrified of something. I'm not some secret food critic. I'm just a man." He chuckled as if at some private joke.

"I'm not terrified of you," she argued.

"Really?" He quirked a brow, still grinning at her.

"Really. I'm just not used to having guys over lately. I don't even know why I invited you."

The smile didn't let up. "So you don't do this for all your brothers' new hires?"

"Not at all." That was the thing that was bothering

her. Even when she was dating, she preferred to spend the night at the man's place, not hers. Her apartment, even though it was small, was her refuge. Her Fortress of Solitude. It was decorated with her favorite pictures of the London and Paris skylines and other places she feared she would never be able to see. There just wasn't money to spend for a trip like that, and her savings always ended up going somewhere else. So her home was off-limits to the men she casually dated.

"You're just sweet, that's all," he replied. "Sweet and brave. I saw you stand up to that man tonight. You weren't scared of him at all, just pissed, but you barely showed it."

"I could have handled him if I hadn't been outnumbered. But I'm not an idiot." She hated how frosty her tone sounded right now, but she was used to defending her actions because her brothers always assumed she couldn't take care of herself.

"I never said you were." He finished off his wine as though it were a glass of water. He was not even buzzed. If she tried to keep up with him, she'd be swaying on her feet in a matter of minutes.

He finished his salad and put his plate in the sink after cleaning it. Something that simple should not have turned her on, but damn, it totally did. Then he took the bottle of wine and put it back in the fridge.

"I can clean up," she said quietly. "You should get

settled. If you have a car, you can park it outside the garage tomorrow."

"Thanks." He started to leave but paused as he noticed the artwork on her wall. He approached one black-and-white photo in particular. It was of the Notre-Dame cathedral in Paris from before the fire that had ravaged it in 2019. The fire had ruined the nine-hundred-year-old structure, devastating the world with its loss. The art and relics inside had been rescued, but some of the priceless stained-glass windows were gone forever.

He reached up to touch the towers, the only parts that hadn't collapsed in the raging inferno. "This was taken before the fire, wasn't it?"

"Yes. My parents went to Paris for their honeymoon. Mom loved the cathedral. She and my dad went to Mass there." Harper's voice thickened as she joined him in front of the framed print.

Pictures were the only way she felt she could relate to the world without headaches. Words were hard to read, which meant she relied heavily on audiobooks to read. But photos truly were worth a thousand words. When she looked at the Notre-Dame, she saw the past, she saw her parents, she saw beauty, faith, and devotion, not necessarily one of religion but to culture. And so much of it was gone, carried away on the winds over the Seine.

"If the Krinar had been there, they could have saved it."

"The Krinar would have tried to save it?" That surprised her.

"Yes, they could have put out much of the flames. The roof was made of nine-hundred-year-old timber, and much of the pews and altars in the church interior were all made of wood. But they could have stopped it if they'd been there. They value human culture." Seth's gaze was solemn and distant in a way that stirred Harper's heart. Whoever this man was, he had a connection to the cathedral on some level, the same way she did because of her parents.

"Were you ever there? Did you see it before the fire?" She didn't stop herself as she reached out and put a hand on his arm.

A world-weary sigh escaped his lips. "I saw it a year before the fire. I never quite got over the reality that what I saw so clearly and looked as if it would last forever is gone." He shook his head and turned toward her. "Thank you for dinner, Harper." He changed the subject so abruptly that she was caught off guard when he leaned down and kissed her.

With a gentle brush of those soft, warm lips over hers, an electric pulse sparked between them. Harper reached up to curl her arms around his neck without thinking. His kiss was a force of nature—raw, sensual, demanding, yet coaxing as he assaulted her senses. Hints of leather and sandalwood mixed with a clean scent that reminded her of fresh laundry and rain. He tasted like the shiraz they'd shared, sweetening her tongue in response.

He groaned and lifted her up by her waist, carrying her to the kitchen counter, where he set her down, bringing her closer to his height. She parted her legs, and he stepped in between them, like an ancient dance they had done a thousand times before. Heat pooled in her belly as a wave of sensual fire carried her away with building pleasure. He threaded a hand in her hair and cupped the back of her head as he devoured her lips.

God, it felt like heaven to be kissed like this, and Seth was a *master*. She was consumed by him, the way his hands roamed reverently down her back to her hips, the way he caressed her hair as though she were precious to him, but his kiss was open-mouthed and raw, dirty in the best possible way. A girl couldn't help but get turned on by this, so much so that it hurt. She whimpered against his lips, desperate in a way she hadn't been in a long time, with a need born of a longing and hunger she'd never felt before now. All of her previous lovers paled in comparison to this man and how he made her feel.

"Bedroom, *now*," she hissed and clawed at his back, wanting to drag him closer to her. He separated their bodies with a soft pop of their lips and cupped her face in his hands.

"You are tempting me in ways I've never been tempted before, but we can't. Not tonight." He licked his lips, and his eyelashes fanned as he blinked almost dazedly, staring intensely at her mouth. "But soon." He whispered the words with such sensual promise that she trembled with excitement.

"Soon," she echoed, still a little stunned that she had just tried to take him to bed when she barely knew him.

"I want to know you, *all* of you. Inside and out." He brushed the pad of his thumb over her lips, and she closed her eyes, savoring his touch. It felt so good she almost cried. Had it really been that long since she had let a man touch her like this? With such intimacy? Not just to get her in bed? Not in the last couple of years, it seemed. The realization made her eyes fill with tears, and before she could stop herself, she was crying.

Seth wrapped his arms around her, and she burrowed against him. Despite the pain inside her, her thoughts were dancing drunkenly around her head. She had held on to so much hurt, so much loss for so many years. Not even her brothers knew what she'd been burying all this time. Yet this man holding her had broken down her defenses with one searing kiss.

"Hush..." He pressed his cheek against the crown of her hair. Then she was carried into her bedroom as though she weighed nothing at all. He set her down and turned to study her dresser.

"Pajamas?" he asked in a soothing voice.

She sniffled, hating how vulnerable she was in that moment, but the tears still flowed freely down her face, and she couldn't make them stop. "Top drawer."

He came over and handed her the pajamas, then pulled back her comforter and sheets. She got up and headed for the bathroom to change, but then she paused at the doorway.

"Please don't go. It's not about sex. I just..." *I just want to be held.* She thought it with such agonizing sorrow that it made her body burn with shame. This level of vulnerability was too much for her.

"I'll stay," he promised and settled back on her bed.

She rushed into the bathroom, changed, brushed her teeth, and wiped a cleansing cloth over her face before she came back into the bedroom. She hoped the puffiness around her eyes would go away soon. There was nothing worse than being near a gorgeous man and looking like crap.

Seth lay on his back now, still fully clothed. He nodded at the empty side of the bed in silent invitation. She came over on anxious tiptoes and climbed into bed, turning off her nightlight. Silence settled in the room. Her heart pounded as she turned toward him, and even though he lay on top of the covers on the other side of her bed, he cocooned her, as if he knew that was exactly what she wanted.

"Good night," she whispered, the tears finally starting to dry upon her cheeks.

"Good night...Queenie."

Ordinarily she never would have let anyone call her that. That belonged to her mother. But when *he* said it, it felt like a promise, a vow, an endearment, and a hundred other intimate things that made her chest tighten and hope blossom inside her.

Whoever you are, Seth, you're already making me fall in love with you. And I swore I'd never do that again.

———

SEF LAY AWAKE LONG AFTER HARPER HAD FALLEN ASLEEP, his mind racing and replaying that kiss over and over. Somehow, the human female had gotten even deeper under his skin than before. He was mere hours into this mission, and already he was losing control of himself. He knew he should contact Arus, perhaps have another guardian assigned to the Kings, but he didn't want another Krinar male anywhere near Harper. The mere thought of it choked him with possessive fury.

Was this how his brother had felt about the president's daughter Bianca? The woman he had betrayed his very position to woo? It was no wonder why they had come to blows over her. Sef had been ordered to remove her from Soren's presence before they became too attached, but it had been too late. Once a Krinar had claimed a charl, they became highly territorial and fiercely possessive.

He was already feeling that way now about Harper. Damn it all.

He held her until just before dawn, then carefully and silently slipped out of her bed and wrote her a note, leaving it in view on the pillow next to her before he left. Instead of returning to his room, however, he pulled out a small device from his jeans that could unlock any door and used it to pass through the garage and into King's Bar.

Sef took an hour placing small microdot cameras in key locations inside the bar and the storeroom. The storeroom was quite large, and ten chairs had been set up for a meeting. By the looks of things, the meeting had already been held. Sef took a mental note of the number for his next report. Ten rebels. Mason, Liam, and eight others, and they had connections to other rebel movements throughout the United States. He needed faces, though. The cameras would pick up their faces, and they could be run through the Krinar databases, which had access to all of the United States' identification systems—not that the Americans were aware of that fact. They could run driver's license photos, passports, thumbprints, criminal mug shots, all of it. Then they could track their past movements and see just how far this infestation had really spread.

He would figure out who the other rebels were and then determine how to proceed. Whatever he did, though, it would hurt Harper. At the very least, her brothers would be taken into Krinar custody for threat evaluation. If they were determined to be beyond rehabilitation, they would have their minds wiped and be reeducated to remove the danger they posed to his people. Such was the way of things.

Harper would lose her brothers, or at least lose the men she had known. They would become different people. It was a harsh punishment, but it was necessary to protect lives, both Krinar and human. The sooner the humans trusted the Krinar and accepted them and let them maintain control of certain things, the better off everyone would be.

Except for Harper. She would never forgive him. That shouldn't have chilled the blood in his veins and made him dread the future, but it did.

4

Harper woke alone, reaching for the warm body that had helped her sleep clear through the night, but she didn't find it. She blinked blearily at the folded piece of paper lying on the pillow where his head had been not too long ago. She opened it up, ignoring the familiar stab of pain at trying to read then note..

Queenie,

Thank you for trusting me last night. I'll see you in the shop later.

Seth

She lay back, staring up at the ceiling, baffled by her behavior last night. He'd punched a man to defend her, so she had invited him to dinner—that was odd enough. Then she'd kissed him and started crying. Then he'd taken her to bed and held her while she slept. How crazy was all that? What the hell had happened to her? And how was Seth so cool with it? That kind of behavior tended to be a hot single guy's worst nightmare, a crying woman who clung to him like a second skin all night.

Wow.

Pushing her covers back, she headed into the bathroom to shower. She halted a second later when she took in a familiar scent. She lifted her arm closer to her nose. Seth's rich, intoxicating scent was still there, clinging to her skin. The thought of washing it off made her frown, but that was insane. Showering would make her feel awake and refreshed. Even as she stripped out of her clothes, she held up her T-shirt and inhaled deeply, his scent calming her. Then she set it in her laundry hamper, ignoring the flicker of regret she felt before she got into the shower.

As the hot water poured down her body, she focused on her work schedule for the day and which clients she knew would be expecting their vehicles. An hour later she was in her gray jumpsuit and ready for anything, even if part of her mind was still lost in last night.

She turned on the shop lights, unlocked the heavy hangar doors, and hit the automatic lift buttons. Morning began to fill the shop, bathing the stained white linoleum floor in gold as the hangar doors rose into the ceiling. She blinked against the skyline and saw a vintage Mustang idling outside. Whoever was behind the wheel of that baby had good taste. She retrieved her sunglasses from her desk and went out to meet the customer. She froze when she saw that it was Seth. He was leaning back against the door now, his legs crossed at his ankles. Was there a handbook out there that taught hot guys how to lean against things, especially cars, in a way that made a woman say "*Damn!*" under her breath?

"Morning, Queenie. You said I could leave my car here? This spot okay?"

She swallowed and smiled, her nerves running riot through her as she walked closer to him. "Uh...yeah. That's fine."

"Sorry about last night. I didn't mean to kiss you without warning like that, and when you..." He couldn't seem to find the right words to describe what had happened.

"Had a meltdown?" Harper offered.

"Not my place to say, but I didn't feel right leaving you alone like that. Must have seemed awkward as hell to you."

She stared down at the toes of her work boots, too mortified to meet his gaze. "I'm more worried about how weird that was for you."

His hand lifted her chin, and their eyes locked. "I liked last night. How about tonight I cook for you?"

His offer stunned her. "You want to do that for me?"

With a teasing wink, he nodded. "Honey, I'll do a lot for an intelligent, pretty woman. What kind of men have you been with that not one has offered to cook you a good meal?"

"Apparently not the right ones." She managed to laugh, even though she was more than a little embarrassed.

"So, you're working here today at the bar?" she asked as he followed her back into the shop.

"I am, but not until five and it's only a three hour shift tonight. You need any help here? No charge, not till I prove myself useful. I like cars. I could help you."

"I bet you could. That car you have outside is a classic, and it has a good purr. That means you either know a good mechanic or you know your way around the car."

"The latter. I've loved machines ever since I was a kid." He glanced around at her shop, openly impressed.

"Well, I won't turn down free help. Alan and Jeff don't work on the weekends. They both have kids and I wanted them to have family time." She also wouldn't turn down the chance to watch Seth today, to smell him, to just be near him. She'd never felt this addiction to a man before, where she wanted to be near him so bad it almost hurt.

"So what's first?" he asked, looking at the three cars in the shop.

"The Ford F150 needs some heavy work on the transmission, and the two Hondas need oil changes, tire rotations, and twenty-four-point systems checks. All the stuff on here." She handed him a colorful checklist. It had pictures of parts and little colored blocks to check on the condition of the parts—red, yellow, and green to indicate how good or bad the part was. This was her secret method of keeping her dyslexia from hurting her business, but it also provided a level of direct simplicity her customers enjoyed, especially if English wasn't their first language.

"What would you like me to do?" Seth asked.

"You can start on the Hondas. It's pretty basic stuff, and it'll give me a chance to see how good you are. I'll tackle the truck." She grabbed her tools and rolled under the truck on her creeper to take a quick look before she got up to start working on the engine.

Once she popped the hood, she quickly lost herself in the world of mechanics. It was a language that made sense to her; there were no headaches here. But even focused on her job, she ended up shooting a glance in Seth's direction, and she bit her lip as she stopped to admire his muscled body. He'd taken off his shirt and now wore only a black tee, which clung to him so tightly she could see the shift of each and every muscle as he cranked a wrench and refilled oil. Now that was a whole other kind of machine she'd like to get her hands on...

"My, my..." A feminine voice came from behind her. Harper jolted and smacked her head on the hood of the truck.

"Ruby," she groaned in a whisper as she faced her desk clerk. Ruby handled the customer paperwork and took payments, and she was early today.

Ruby leaned back against the welcome desk. She was forty-five but always looked a decade younger. She wore a short skirt and high heels and a tight top. She was a single mother with a twelve-year-old son, and she was also a hopeless romantic. Harper adored her, but she did not care for the way Ruby was eyeing Seth.

"Who's that?" Ruby whispered loudly. "Please tell me he's single."

Harper wiped her oily hands on a rag and came over to Ruby's desk so Seth wouldn't overhear their conversation.

"He's working at the bar for a while. He's helping this morning for free. So hands off," she warned.

Ruby swept her dark-blonde hair over her shoulders and grinned at Harper. "Oh my God, *please* tell me you are hitting that. Hard. It would be a crime to go to bed alone when you could have someone like him to keep you company."

"You don't know anything about him," Harper countered.

"What's there to know about him, other than in the biblical sense?"

Heat flushed Harper's face. "We only just met, and...it's complicated."

Ruby cut her off. "Honey, there's no such thing as complicated with a man like that." She took one more lingering look before she sat back down at the reception desk. Seth glanced their way, and Ruby waved at him.

"I'm Ruby," she shouted. "Nice to meet you, handsome."

Harper almost slapped her palm against her forehead, but Seth laughed and winked at Ruby.

"Seth Jackson. Nice to meet you, ma'am." He then returned to work on the Honda.

"Ma'am," Ruby echoed, her face turning red as a cherry as she fanned herself. "He has manners, at least. Not like those louts in town who think belching is the same thing as a *please* and *thank you*."

Harper groaned in further embarrassment. "Ruby..."

"What? You know you love me, hon."

"God help me, I do." Harper shook her head. Ruby was like a young favorite aunt, and a wild one at that. She was vivacious and outgoing, sexy and fun. Everything Harper felt she wasn't and it was nice to be around sometimes. Ruby reminded her how to have fun and be a woman every now and then.

"Harper, honey, little tip. Unzip the top of your jumpsuit—show off the goods if you want to get his attention," Ruby muttered to her and then focused on her computer screen.

Harper glanced down at her jumpsuit. She'd never given any thought to looking sexy while on the job. When she was working, the last thing she needed was a man tripping over himself just because she'd decided to show off a little bit of cleavage. But Seth didn't strike her as the type of man to trip over himself.

She worked for a few more minutes before she reached up and pulled the zipper on her suit down. She had on a tank top underneath, and she had to admit, it did give a good view of her breasts. Feeling like an idiot, she waited for Seth to notice, but his back was to her as he bent over the engine of the second Honda. She walked over to stand beside him and put her hands on her hips, which pumped her chest up a bit more.

"How's it going?" She tried to sound casual.

God, this is so stupid. What the hell am I doing?

Seth shot her a glance and then did a double take, his eyes fixed on her cleavage.

"Better now," he said, his gaze burning with a desire that sent her own body into a hungry spiral of need.

What the hell was happening? He was making her

nuts with just a look. Maybe they both just needed to get it out of their system?

"I'll...be in my office for a few minutes." She wasn't sure why she was telling him. Did she really want him to follow her? Yeah, she did. She rushed to her office, leaving open the door that led to the hall between the bar and the garage, her heart hammering. A minute later he came inside and closed the door.

"Lock it," she said, her body throbbing now.

He flicked the lock in place and stared at her, eyes locked like a predator finding its prey. The feeling was mutual. Her feet seemed to drift along inches above the floor as she moved to him just as he came to her. She ripped at his shirt, pulling it off violently while he yanked down the zipper of her jumpsuit. She shrugged her arms out of her sleeves and pulled her tank top off, leaving her top bare except for the black lace bra she wore.

"You are so fucking gorgeous." He reached up to brush a thumb over her nipple through the fabric of her bra.

This attraction between them was as tumultuous as a summer storm and just as maddening as it swept through them both on a dizzying current of arousal. Her womb clenched so hard she clamped her thighs together.

"Don't say no, not this time," she begged as she ran her palms along his hard chest. He was so warm, so virile. She felt almost drunk, being so close to the pleasure she sensed instinctively he could give her.

"I should," he growled, the sound rumbling deep from within his chest and into her. "But I can't. If I could, I would fuck you for days." He lowered his head to hers, the kiss so gentle compared to his rough words. "I want to make you scream my name. I want to brand myself on you, feel you clamp down around my cock and beg for more." The pictures he painted in her mind were carnal, raw, and utterly...devastatingly perfect.

"Yes please, do it," she moaned against him, and their hands roamed wildly, tearing at each other's clothes, pulling away fabric.

Her jumpsuit ended up in pieces on the floor, and he tore her shorts down her legs and tossed them away. Then he pulled her up and set her down on the desk, scattering paperwork to the floor. She started to laugh, but he hooked his fingertips in her panties and ripped them clean off. It didn't even hurt. She whimpered as he laid her down on her back on her desk, pushing her knees wide as he stared down at her exposed sex. She stared up at him in turn, tongue-tied as he ran a fingertip down her slit, slowly stroking her. She burned in the wake of that touch. He slipped his finger between his own lips and licked it clean. His eyes rolled back in his head as he growled at her taste.

"Like sweet wine." He lowered himself over her,

and before she was ready, he laid his mouth over her core.

His tongue teased her, keeping her prisoner to the sweetest pleasure she'd ever felt. He licked her clit as though it were a ripe berry and swiped boldly at her with his tongue. She'd never really understood why they called it being "eaten out," but she felt it now, the way he was *consuming* all of her in that moment, heart, body, and soul. All of it seemed pulled together into the epicenter between her thighs. Her fingers roamed through his hair, the silky thickness of the strands tickling her skin.

"You like that, honey? You like my tongue inside you?" His eyes met hers, and her body leaped with a sharp pang of hunger, and then at something more.

"Oh fuck!" she hissed as a climax shot through her, shattering her. She went limp on the desk, with no strength left in her thighs to pull them together.

"Still want me?" Seth asked in a husky voice.

She nodded weakly, wanting to die from pleasure as she imagined how good it would feel to have him ramming inside her while she still quaked with the aftershocks of an orgasm. "Yes. God, yes. No condom. I'm clean and on the pill."

"I'm clean too." He unzipped his jeans, and her eyes widened at the sight of him. He wasn't just big. He was too big.

She tried to sit up. "Wait..."

"Easy," he whispered and chuckled as he moved between her thighs again. "We'll go slow. You can take me, Queenie. Trust me."

"Okay," she sighed as he cupped her face with one hand, and then he captured her lips with his. He guided his cock with his other hand and pushed inside. She didn't mean to, but she tensed and panted as the stretching invasion made her whimper, and she bit his lip by accident.

"Sorry!" she gasped, but he moved his mouth to her neck and murmured for her to relax.

There was a sharp pain as he gave her a love bite. No, wait—it was more than that. And then...then the world was spinning, and she fell over the edge into bliss as Seth thrust deep inside her. Their hips collided as he sank deep into her. She screamed in ecstasy, but he silenced her with a dirty kiss that only made her need him more.

"Hang on, honey," he warned, then started fucking her, raw, hard, like he needed to pound them together like two metals burning hot against one another in a blacksmith's forge.

She struggled to breathe, but each breath escaped her lips as a desperate cry for more. She dug her fingers into his shoulders, clawing at him as he plunged into her. This primal joining seemed to go on forever, and she didn't want it to stop. Her muscles clamped down around his shaft, trying to draw him in deeper. Each stroke, each piston of his hips was better than the last, until it was all too much. Her body overloaded and she came, stars in her eyes. For a second their faces were inches apart. His blue eyes seemed tinged with gold, and he licked his bloody lips. Why was there blood on his lips? *Wait, the bite...*

He bucked and roared her name as he released himself deep inside her. She shuddered beneath him as he thrust into her a few more times, his body shaking, before she drifted to sleep on the desk. The last sensation she had was of him leaning over her, still buried inside her as he licked the tender throbbing spot on her neck.

5

Harper's blood on his tongue was the most intoxicating rush he'd ever experienced. It felt like his body was vibrating with new power and deep, carnal longings that were a mix of lusting for blood and the intimacy of Harper's body. But a small part of him was being ripped apart with guilt as well. Between claiming her body and tasting her blood, he had made a terrible mistake. He knew many Krinar could taste human blood and enjoy the highs given from human strangers, but now that he knew Harper, and was fascinated by her taste, touch, and thoughts, she was irresistible. There was no way he would ever let her go now.

She belonged to him. Sef would just have to face that new reality.

He would take her as his charl, and if she tried to

resist, he would fuck her just like this, giving her such pleasure that she would never want to leave him. He would spoil her rotten, give her everything she wanted. How could she say no to that? The thought made him grin as he placed a kiss on her neck. She sighed and murmured something dreamily as he pulled out of her, but he knew his saliva was now in her bloodstream, making her high, for lack of a better word. She would be tired for a few hours and need to rest.

The drugging effects of Krinar saliva had evolved as a means to subdue the lonar, a primate species on their home world of Krina. The lonar possessed a crucial hemoglobin in their blood that the Krinar lacked in sufficient quantities but needed to survive. And the Krinar had survived, excelled even, as the lonar had declined. They had developed a synthetic substitute, but other contingencies had been planned for long ago, including interfering in the development of other species. Humans had evolved from one such mission, perhaps their most successful one. The similarity in lonar and human blood made sucking from a human an intoxicating rush.

He swore he could feel his own blood sing as he licked his lips, but he forced himself to focus on caring for his female. He carried her off the desk and over to the couch that stretched along one side of the office wall perpendicular to her desk. He covered her with a fleece blanket and placed a small pillow beneath her head. Her strawberry-blonde hair had escaped her ponytail during their frenzied mating, and he brushed it out of her face.

"Seth," she murmured, though her eyes remained closed.

"I'm here."

Her eyes opened, and he knelt down by her face.

"What we did, I've never done that. I mean sex, sure, but we're strangers. I don't just do that, you know?" She yawned, covering her mouth with a fist. Fuck, she was adorable.

"We aren't strangers, Queenie. We're friends." He had rarely used that word to describe a female, but it was true. She was a friend. In this short amount of time, he'd been more himself than he'd ever been, even though he was pretending to be someone else.

She yawned again. "Friends?"

"Yes." He stroked a fingertip down her nose, and her lips curved in a smile.

"Wake me in an hour then, will you, pal?" she asked, her eyes closing again.

Sef smirked. "Of course." He had no intention of waking her. She still needed time to get over the effects of his saliva. The first exposure was always the strongest. He had also felt the calluses on her hands and seen how exhausted she had been last night. No, he was going to let her sleep. He would finish her work for her so she might have the evening off.

He left her in her office to sleep and returned to the auto shop.

"Where's Harper?" Ruby stood from her desk, giving him a clear once-over.

"In her office resting. Please don't wake her. I'll take care of her work today."

"I bet you will, handsome." Ruby chuckled and sat back down at her desk. Ruby was quiet for a long while, watching him as he finished. The press of her gaze on the back of his head put his nerves on edge. Finally, when he faced Ruby, instead of smiling she was coldly serious.

"See, the thing is, if you hurt her, in *any* way, it won't be her brothers you have to worry about. Harper is special."

Sef wiped his hands, dropped the hood down on the Ford F150, and came over to Ruby's desk.

"I know. I've never met anyone like her." *Not on Krina or Earth,* he added silently.

He eyed the paperwork on the desk in front of Ruby and saw several notes scattered with poorly scribbled handwriting. It didn't match the clean-cut precision of the paper Ruby was writing on. Sef picked up one of the notes, trying to read it. It looked something like human shorthand, but it wasn't.

"Ruby, is something wrong? She didn't want me seeing her handwriting last night. I sensed it really upset her." He stared at the human woman before him, unleashing the full intensity of his focus on her.

Ruby's gaze darted away from him. "She...doesn't like talking about it."

"Ruby, I don't want to hurt her, but if I don't understand this"—he waved a little scrap of paper in the air —"then I might hurt her accidentally."

Ruby exhaled, and then in a very quiet voice she said, "Harper has a severe case of dyslexia. She's always had trouble reading and writing, but she's a genius."

"What do you mean by *genius*?"

"Well, like this for instance." Ruby opened her desk drawer and pulled out several rolled-up blueprints. She unrolled one on her desk, and it set his heart racing. The blueprint showed clear designs for a flying spacecraft. It was similar to the technology used by the Krinar. Harper had written some equations, messily, that relied on antigravity force field technology.

"She's been working on these the last few years, based on what little information she's been able to get about the Ks' ships. I mean, there's a whole station that does nothing but theorize and speculate about how their stuff works. She has an instinct for what bits are bunk and which are on the money. She understands the science, but she can't write the formulas without help, and no one in Lawrence is smart enough to help her. And because of her condition, she can't exactly chat with other folks on the forums about it. That's why she's stuck in the shop all day. I do my best to help, but I never got past calculus in school myself, so..." She blushed. "But Harper, even though she faced tough times growing up, she's really intelligent. I bet you anything she wished she was working on these all day instead. But it's just not in the cards, you know?" Ruby waved at the little Post-its scattered on the desk. "I swear I can't read what she writes most of the time. I think it hurts her too much to even write these few notes."

The image of her face, the look of terror when the asshole from the bar had demanded she write his order down, and her reluctance to give him her notepad all made sense. She didn't want him to know about her dyslexia.

"But she can draw?" he asked, looking down at the blueprints again.

"Yes, quite well."

Sef examined the ship's sleek design. The mechanical components were simple, uncomplicated, and full of understated brilliance. Granted, there were gaps in her knowledge, assumptions that had been made on how K technology worked, but still... If she didn't suffer from dyslexia, she might make some incredible inventions, ones his people would be thrilled to help her bring to life.

"These look like Krinar ships." His guardian training put him somewhat on edge, wondering if perhaps she had been given access to forbidden tech to be this close to being right.

"She's obsessed with their tech, watches everything she can on YouTube about it. Harper can't stop talking about their designs. She watches all of the news on them, though she has to turn it off when Mason and Liam are around."

"Not K friendly?" he asked, keeping his tone casual.

"Mason and Liam?" Ruby snorted. "You could say that. Can't blame them, though, what with losing their parents the way they did. Boys don't handle tragedy well. Women, we either cry or we bury it so deep it never surfaces again. Boys, they bottle it up in a way that when they get shaken too much they just explode." Ruby made an exploding motion with her hands.

"I suppose that's true." Sef couldn't help but think of the way Harper had clung to him last night, the way she'd cried.

It was so clear to him now that something inside her had finally struggled to the surface, all because she'd responded to him. He'd wanted to show her tenderness, show her that he was capable of protecting and caring for her. Her tears would have been viewed as a weakness to most males, especially humans, but to him, it was evidence of a strong heart, one which bore such great pain but could also feel great joy. Sef wanted to give her a million reasons to feel such joy—he just had to find a way.

Ruby hastily rolled the blueprints back up and tucked them into the bottom left drawer of the desk. "I should put these back."

"Thank you for showing them to me." He glanced at the door that led to Harper's office. "I suppose I should wake her up."

Ruby chuckled.

"Do what you need to, handsome. I'll be heading home. I'll lock up."

Sef thanked her again and entered Harper's office. She was still asleep, and would be for hours. He grinned and carefully scooped her up, blanket and all, and carried her back to her apartment.

He then went to shower and change for tonight's shift at the bar. Once he was clean, he sat down in a chair and pulled up the hologram footage of the bar. He sped through several feeds until he saw Mason and Liam entering the storeroom alone. He slowed the playback down to real time. The brothers were speaking quietly, so he increased the volume.

"He wants to meet tonight?" Mason asked. Liam double-checked that the storeroom was empty before he answered.

"Yeah. He sent an encrypted message an hour ago. But..." Liam's face darkened.

"But?" Mason asked.

"But this feels like one step too far for me. He's a radical. We want freedom from the Ks. He wants them dead, and he doesn't care about collateral damage. I don't think we should work with him."

Mason crossed his arms and leaned back against the storeroom door. "That bad, huh?"

"Worse."

"Then fuck him. We aren't going to get rid of monsters by becoming monsters. But..."

"But?" Liam prompted.

"What if it turns out there is no other way? I don't want to speak lightly of it, but what if we have no other option?"

"You can't be serious."

"The Ks have no reason to listen to us waving signs and distributing leaflets. They can do pretty much whatever they want, whenever they want. The only way they'll leave is if we're too much trouble for them to bother sticking around."

Sef zoomed in on Mason, seeing the concern on his face. For a moment Sef wavered in his determination to expose and capture them. These men simply wanted freedom, but they were going to align themselves with far more dangerous men.

"Thing is, if we're on the inside, we can steer them away from their crazier ideas. Try to get them to focus on the chaos and not the casualties. Let's just hear them out before we decide to give them the boot or not," Mason said to Liam. "He'll be here at four in the morning."

Liam frowned. "I don't like it, but fine. I'll tell the others."

Sef stopped the feed and sent a copy of the conversation to Arus. A few minutes later his friend contacted him, his face hovering in a crystal-clear hologram.

"I viewed the recording. How do you wish to proceed?"

"I wish to monitor the situation further. We need to know the identity of the man the King brothers intend to meet. He sounds like a far more dangerous threat, and we need to know how many others he has ready to support his cause. I will keep you informed."

"And their sister? You've made no reports on her." Arus's astute observations made Sef frown.

"I am monitoring her as well, but she doesn't seem to harbor anti-K tendencies like her brothers. Her file stated her parents died during the initial resistance when we arrived on Earth. A bridge was bombed with them on it. Can you find out more about them? It may help me with the brothers."

"I can look into it," Arus said.

"Good." Sef paused, thinking of Harper's blueprints. Arus didn't miss his hesitation.

"What else do you want to tell me?"

"It's the girl. She's..." How could he describe

Harper? She was brave, brilliant, compassionate, tempting...

"Yes?"

"She has a neurological condition called dyslexia. A rather severe form, I understand. Could you have someone research it? She is a brilliant mechanical engineer. I think we could find her useful."

"For a human, I'm sure she is. But useful to us? How?"

"She seems to have an uncanny understanding of our technology. Some of her insights are so accurate I assumed she somehow had gained access to our ships, but they're based on little more than secondhand observations."

"That seems highly unlikely."

"I agree. But there is an untapped potential there worth exploring. I believe that if I could help her with her dyslexia, she might be able to work alongside Korum." Korum was a master inventor and a good friend of his. If it turned out Harper could be trusted, she might be of value to his people and hers.

"Interesting." Arus stroked his chin. "I suppose if she's as gifted as you say, she could help bridge relations with the humans. I will speak with our doctors about what we know about dyslexia and forward whatever information I find about the King parents."

"Thank you, Arus." Sef ended the call and readied himself for work.

Tonight he would find a way to distract Harper while his cameras recorded the meeting her brothers hosted. She would be none the wiser. While this should have put him at ease, instead it left a lingering tension coiled like a snake ready to strike. He was not betraying Harper, he told himself. He didn't owe her anything...or did he?

He'd drunk her blood, had claimed her body in the most primal way possible, and an invisible bond had begun to form between them. The thought scared him, but it also fascinated him. He suspected this was why his brother had reacted so madly when it came to his human, Bianca. The need to protect, to possess, to pleasure Harper grew steadily stronger within him, and he could not see a way to stop it or even slow it down.

We are bound, Queenie. Bound by the body...and perhaps much more.

6

Late-afternoon sunlight warmed Harper's skin, and she stretched out on her bed and smiled. The fragments of the most wonderful dream still clung to her, shimmering like the effervescent strands of a magical web.

She lay on the back of the truck bed, the sun heating her body as she watched the clouds move above her. They changed and morphed as she watched them. Soft, sensual lips were at her neck, pressing teasing kisses against her. Her lover chuckled as she squirmed beneath his tender seduction.

"We can't stay too long..." She threaded her fingers through his blond hair. The light caught and shone on those golden strands.

"We have forever, Queenie," he promised.

Then the dream changed. The bridge had collapsed. Her

parents' car sank below the surface of the river as sleek silver alien ships continued to appear in the skies. Bubbles frothed at the surface where the car had landed, and soon there was nothing but black water.

Bleak despair jolted Harper awake. She lay panting and shaking as the old grief of five years ago came back in full force. She scrubbed her eyes with her fists, and her hands came away coated with tears. Choking down a sob, she couldn't get herself to move for several minutes. It had been a long time since that dream had haunted her.

Harper drew in a slow breath, counting to ten in her head, and she reclaimed a sense of calm. When she looked down at herself, she gasped. She wore only a bra, the uncomfortable lacy one she never wore except for dates where she thought she might go home with the guy.

What the—?

The memories of that morning came rushing back with an electric force.

She and Seth had screwed like bunnies in her office.

Had that really happened?

Holy shit...it had.

She buried her face in her hands, mortified. Seth had to think she was too easy and just slept with anyone. She wanted to hide in her sock drawer and never leave her apartment again.

Wait... She was in her apartment? Harper remembered falling asleep in her office. So how did she end up back here?

Harper ducked into the bathroom and froze at what she saw in the mirror. She had a hickey on her neck, a big one, where Seth had bitten her, and her hair was a messy tumble of color. Her hips had slight bruises from where he'd grasped her as he'd thrust into her, though they didn't hurt.

"What's wrong with you?" she asked her reflection. "You can't just jump a guy like that."

She frowned at herself for another moment before she turned on the water and got into the shower.

To distract herself, she focused instead on the work she hadn't finished. She needed to call Ruby, who had no doubt already gone home for the day since she usually left at after three p.m. on the weekends.

When she returned to the shop, she found all the cars completed, even the Ford. Ruby's desk was clean and organized, which meant the cars were all finished and ready to be picked up tomorrow morning.

Had Seth done all of this? That was the only explanation. She knew her brothers couldn't have done it. They couldn't do much more than change the oil, which meant it must have been Seth, but he had promised to wake her up in an hour. She checked the wall clock at the back of the garage. It was nearly four in the afternoon. She'd slept away most of the day.

Harper entered the bar and scanned the room until she saw Seth. He wore a dark blue T-shirt that clung to him like a second skin, and the way his body fit those jeans... She bit her lip as she stared at his ass, remembering how it had felt to have the full focus of his thrusting body against her and how she'd never wanted it to end, even if it had killed her.

Seth stood behind the bar with Neil, pouring beers and laughing at something Neil said. Liam moved behind the bar and slapped Seth's shoulder in greeting as he opened one of the cash registers. Mason came out of the storeroom with a new case of beer and nodded at Seth, who nodded back.

Harper imagined for one minute that this was normal, that she could come here every afternoon and see this. Seth working at the bar, that wicked, playful curve of his lips promising pleasure just for her, and the sound of his rich laughter ringing like church bells. This could be just any other day...in a perfect life...an *almost* perfect life, if her parents had been here to see it.

Her eyes burned with tears, but she couldn't look away. Everything she cared about was in this room. Seth was a part of her world now, whether she wanted him to be or not. He was slipping through the chinks in her armor.

"Hey, Harper!" Jessie joined her, an empty drink tray balanced on one hip.

"Hey." Harper shot her friend a smile. "How's he doing?" She pointed discreetly toward Seth.

"Pretty good. He's all smiles and charm, but he doesn't let any of the customers get the wrong idea, you know? To be a good waiter, you have to balance the charm, or you'll have some creep palming your ass." Jessie wrinkled her nose in disgust.

"I'm glad he's working out." Harper turned her attention back on him. As if he sensed her focus, he looked right at her, and the smile he flashed grew a hundred times brighter. It was a smile meant only for her. The love bite on her neck tingled, and she reached up instinctively to touch it, then carefully pulled her hair back down to cover it. If her brothers saw that, she'd be in major trouble.

"How long will he be sticking around?" Jessie asked. "He's already bringing in way more business." Jessie pointed to the tables full of women who were all gazing in adoration at Seth.

A flash of envy prickled beneath her skin. It was like those women had never seen a good-looking man before. Her brothers were good-looking—even she could admit that from an objective standpoint—but the women in the bar had eyes only for her man.

He isn't mine—or is he? She wanted him to be, but how did she even *start* that conversation? They'd just had crazy-hot sex in her office, but they hadn't discussed a relationship. What if all this was only physical to him? And why the hell was she letting it be more than physical for her? She knew better than to want to fall in love with someone like Seth. But he made her want to believe in that wild, crazy, love-at-first-sight kind of passion again.

"Harper? Hello? Earth to Harper," Jessie teased.

"Hmmm?" She turned her focus back to her friend.

"Just go talk to him," Jessie encouraged.

Harper decided to take her friend's advice and moved toward the bar.

"Hey," Seth greeted as she reached him.

"Hey." She blushed all the way to the roots of her hair. She nodded toward the storeroom. "Can we talk?"

"Sure."

He followed her into the room behind the *Employees Only* sign, making sure neither of her brothers got suspicious as to why.

"So." She stared down at her Converse shoes, suddenly wishing she'd worn something more attractive. She didn't own any high heels since she didn't see much use in them. Now she wished she had a closetful of fancy clothes.

"So..." Seth stepped forward and gripped her hips in his hands, a move that seemed so natural to him, as though he could grab and hold her like that anytime he wanted, and damned if she didn't like it. He moved a hand up to her neck, brushing back her hair to expose the hickey she'd been trying to hide. He frowned.

"I bit you too hard," he said. "I will be gentler next time."

She covered his hand with hers, their gazes locking. "Don't be. I liked it just the way you did it. I never knew I had an erogenous zone there."

He trailed his fingers over the sensitive mark. "Most men don't know how to properly arouse a woman there. It's a combination of factors—pressure from a bite and feathering ticklish light kissing."

"Well, whatever it is, you sure know how to do it." She wasn't sure if she liked knowing that he'd developed his seduction into a science.

"I pay attention to a woman when I'm with her, especially you." Seth's words seemed to reassure her. She couldn't judge him for having a past, no more than he could judge her. Fair was fair. They weren't virgins, so they shouldn't be acting like they were.

"I don't want to sound crazy or clingy or anything... but after what happened this morning, I guess I just want to know." She bit her bottom lip. "Where do we go from here?" She wanted to smack herself. That sounded pathetically clingy, and she was not a woman to ever be like that.

"Where do you want to go?" Seth's eyes were hot with hunger.

"I…" She was now staring at his mouth. "As crazy as it sounds, I think I want to be in a relationship."

His hands on her hips tightened, and he urged her closer until the heat of his body radiated against her, even though they were barely touching. He leaned down, his mouth a bare inch from hers.

"Then let's say we are."

"Okay." She closed the distance, needing to feel him, to steal a kiss that she wanted more than her next breath.

She wasn't disappointed. He took possession of her lips, and their tongues dueled for pleasure as she wrapped her arms around his neck. He cupped her head, his fingers entwined in the strands of her hair as he exquisitely made love to her mouth. It was a kiss that went on for what felt like days and could have gone on for years for all she cared.

Before she realized it, he had pinned her against the wall of the storeroom, his body completely trapping hers. She couldn't escape him—not that she wanted to. She loved the feel of his hard chest against hers, the weight of his thighs as he rocked his hips into her, letting her feel his hard arousal dig into her belly. She whimpered as he unbuttoned her shorts and slid a hand under the waistline of her panties. Seth pressed the heel of his hand against her clit. She bit her lip hard so she wouldn't cry out at the intense rush of excitement.

"You want me to get you off, honey? Right here in the storeroom, with everyone just outside?"

"Yes!" she gasped. "Please, Seth, do it..." She didn't care that she was begging, because his fingertips were stroking her inner folds, playing with her, making her squirm and buck against his grip.

"Ask me, honey. I want to hear those words come from your pretty lips." His voice deepened. She could tell he was hungry to be inside her, but he was already giving her the pleasure she craved.

"Please, get me off."

"I'm already doing that," he growled. "What else?"

"I need you to...fuck me."

"There's my naughty girl." He plunged two fingers deep inside her, stretching her, and she moaned. He pumped steadily, then curled his fingers, finding a spot that made her see stars when he rubbed it. Then he added a third finger, but it still wasn't enough.

"Please...I want you, not your hand." She dug her fingers into his shoulders, keeping him close as he continued to play with her.

"You sure? I won't be gentle. Can't be now," he warned.

She nodded. "Need you. Now. Don't care." She was panting, barely able to breathe around her words as her body vibrated with need.

Suddenly she was facing the wall, her shorts and panties tugged down to her ankles. He kicked her legs apart, and his cock rubbed against her entrance as he used one hand to guide himself to her aching, wet folds. He teased her, letting her brace herself as he gripped her by the back of her neck with his other hand.

"Just fuck me!" she hissed, pushing her ass against his groin and arching her back.

"Fuck!" he snarled back and rammed his cock into her. She arched up on her tiptoes as he filled her completely. The sudden invasion burned, but she liked it, liked the way it felt when he was unapologetic in his lust, because it made hers burn that much hotter.

He lightly squeezed the back of her neck, just enough to hold her in place, like a male would any female who might struggle to get free, but she was right where she wanted to be, feeling this beautiful man fuck her into oblivion. He rode her hard from behind, giving her that edge of almost pain that made everything around her seem to blur and then jerk into sharp focus over and over.

Being with him was like losing her sanity and finding her mind all at once, and all the while her body shattered over and over with peaking waves of pleasure as a climax roared through her. Her blood pounded so hard against her ears that she couldn't hear anything above the whooshing noise for several long seconds. Seth's hands gripped her hips as he pumped into her another dozen times before he lowered his head and sank his teeth into her neck, not breaking the skin.

The light bite sent aftershocks deeper through her womb, and she felt herself clenching around his cock as he filled her. She felt amazing...and knowing he'd just come inside her, hard like that and she'd have to go and monitor the bar with a part of him still within her...it was a dirty, wonderful thought that should have mortified her. Instead, she managed a drowsy and contented smile.

She leaned against the wall for support, watching him as he removed a paper towel from one of the storage racks to clean himself up. She bit her lip as he fixed his jeans and approached her. He stroked his fingers down her spine and along the curve of her bottom before he took the time to clean her too. Then he handed her back her panties and shorts. She slipped them up, and now her face decided to flush as the reality of it all sank in.

What the hell was wrong with her that she just kept jumping this man at every opportunity?

"Hey," he whispered softly, pulling her back into his arms. "You okay? I wasn't too...?"

"No, I'm good. Just...I don't do this normally. I don't... What is it about you that makes me so crazy?" She asked the question more to herself than to him.

"I don't know, but it's the same for me. I don't just grab any girl and fuck her like that." He chuckled, his rich baritone voice turning her into melted butter inside. "You're something special, Harper." He leaned down to kiss the tip of her nose, and she wriggled closer to him, pressing herself against his body and breathing in his dark masculine scent, now edged with sweat. Damn...he was like catnip to her.

They broke apart when someone banged a fist on the storeroom door.

"Hey, why's the door locked?" Jessie's muffled voice asked.

Harper gazed up at him bashfully. Seth's smirk wasn't arrogant—rather, it was strangely charming, as if he was pleased about what had just happened.

"You ready for me to cook for you tonight?" he asked. "I get off at eight." His eyes shimmered with heat as he gave her hips a gentle squeeze.

She leaned into him a little, wishing for another kiss but knowing they didn't have time. Not yet. "I'd like that."

"Good. Let me go out first. You wait here a minute. I don't need your brothers throwing me out if they see me kissing you."

"Agreed."

Harper giggled, feeling wildly happy at the thought of tonight. She hadn't had a date in about a year. Seth left the storeroom, and she counted a full minute before she exited, but Jessie was waiting for her.

"Storeroom hookup, huh? Not bad. Never thought

you had it in you." Jessie's brown eyes twinkled, and she nudged Harper playfully in the ribs.

"What?" Harper asked. "We just talked."

Jessie glanced around as though checking to see if anyone was listening.

"*And?*"

"And what?" Harper blinked in confusion. "There was no *and*."

Jessie rolled her eyes. She wasn't buying it for a second.

"Okay, fine, we hooked up."

"And the truth shall set you free. So is it just casual, then?"

"Well, we talked about maybe dating," Harper admitted. She and Seth had gone about their relationship totally backward, but maybe that was okay.

"Dating is good. Usually that comes before the sex, though." Jessie tightened the strings on her small black apron and checked that her order pad was there. "You need to date, Harper. I know it's been hard, and that dick of a boyfriend didn't make things easier, but now is the time to open yourself up again. Get back out there, you know?"

Jessie was right. She'd been hiding for too long, letting her fear of intimacy keep her from being happy. It was time to change things. She watched Seth taking orders at a table and grinned as she studied his tall, muscled body and how perfectly he filled out his jeans.

Tonight was going to be amazing, she just knew it.

————

Sef waited for Harper to head back to the garage, and then he cornered Jessie at the bar.

"I need your advice," he said as they cleaned glasses.

"Shoot."

"Well, I'm cooking Harper dinner tonight. What's her favorite food?" He mentally ran through an extensive list of things he could prepare. Unlike his twin, Sef had a knack for culinary skills.

"Hmm..." Jessie tapped her chin thoughtfully. "Grilled cheese, maybe? Tomato soup? It was something her mom used to make for her and her brothers."

"Grilled...*cheese*?" Sef frowned. Such a simple dish. How could he show off his talents with such an uncomplicated meal? Perhaps that was all she needed, a good hearty meal that would bring back happy memories of her family.

"Keep it simple. You know what they say—it's the thought that counts," Jessie said. "Just ...just don't hurt her, okay? She's one of my best friends. She's been through a lot since K-Day."

Sef nodded. "I know about her parents."

"It's not just her parents." Jessie's eyes were serious, and the girl looked wise beyond her years. "She deserves a man who will love her and cherish her. I know that you just blew into town, but we have rules about her. No heartbreaking allowed. You do and you'll deal with me. Whatever is left of you after that, Mason and Liam can dispose of."

Sef was rather impressed by the small human's fierce loyalty to his possible future charl, and while Jessie could not harm him physically, her words made it clear what was at stake.

"I understand," he promised Jessie. "She's special. Once-in-a-lifetime special."

And coming from him, after eight thousand years of being without a long-term companion, that was saying something. But Jessie would never know that.

She relaxed her intense posture and dropped her hands from her hips. "Good. Just so long as we're on the same page. So if you're cooking for her tonight, you should do it on the roof. There's a stairwell along the back. It's pretty nice up there. Romantic even, if you spruce it up a bit."

"Thank you. That's an excellent idea." Sef was already making plans on how he would seduce his little human.

7

Sef worked the remainder of his three hour shift, collecting his tips, which, from the look on Jessie's face, was considered an impressive haul. He had no need for the money, so what wasn't used during his mission would be donated to a human charity. As soon as Katie arrived to take over the late shift that started at eight, he returned to his apartment and found a message on his communications system from Arus confirming Sef's plan to monitor the meeting tonight.

He retrieved the fabricator from the vent by the front door and screwed the vent cover back on before he headed up to the roof. It was dark, but the sky was clear. The stargazing tonight would be incredible. Jessie was right. The roof would be romantic, and he was going to make it even better.

Working quickly, Sef used the fabricator to form two comfortable lawn chairs with plush cushions and a fire pit. Then he made several strings of light and hung them from some poles left behind by a construction crew. He positioned the chairs close to the fire pit and made plaid throw blankets for them.

With a satisfied look around, he returned to his apartment to shower and change. Then he cooked a meal and carried it upstairs to the roof in covered dishes. Now it was time to retrieve his female.

His heart was beating a little faster than usual as he knocked on Harper's door.

"Just a sec!"

A moment later the door was flung wide, and his heart leaped into his throat at the sight of her. She wore a soft dark-green dress that stopped just above her knees and tan cork wedge sandals that made her a few inches taller, though still much shorter than him. Her strawberry-blonde hair was down around her shoulders in luscious waves and soft curls. She even wore a bit of makeup. Not that she needed any, but her smoky eyes seemed more mysterious now, with hints of shadow around them. She wore a gold locket around her neck that rested against her collarbone. For some reason, glimpsing the gold trinket against her pale-gold skin made him thirsty to sink his teeth into her skin and taste her.

"Do I look okay?" Harper reached out to touch her hair, her face reddening.

"You look exquisite." His voice came out a little hoarse.

"Thanks." Her breathless reply made him think back to that morning in her office and the way she had moaned and begged him for pleasure in that same breathless way.

"Dinner is up on the roof," he said. Her brows lifted.

"The roof?"

"Yeah, come on." He held out his hand and felt a rush of triumph when she placed her hand in his.

They climbed the stairs, and he opened the door that led to the roof and stepped aside for her to walk out ahead of him. Strings of lights illuminated the roof. The fire in the pit was already crackling merrily.

"Oh my..." Harper walked over to the chairs and stroked the thick woolen blankets. "This is incredible." She spun around, her green skirt flaring a little to reveal a tantalizing glimpse of her thighs. Sef almost lost himself for a moment.

"You like it?"

Her head bobbed, sending her hair in a cascade of color around her face. "It's wonderful."

He pointed at the chairs. "Have a seat."

When she was sitting down, he retrieved a covered

plate and passed her a glass of wine. She removed the cover, and her eyes gleamed.

"Real cheese?"

"Yeah, and this." He handed her a bowl and removed the covering. "Tomato bisque."

He'd tried to go above and beyond, using a blend of expensive cheddars and pepper jack on the grilled cheese. The bisque had a dollop of sour cream and dill on top, spiced lightly with oregano.

"Who told you?" Her face turned to his as he sat down in the chair beside her with his own plate and bowl.

"Jessie. She didn't want me to screw this up." He chuckled and waited for her to take a bite. She sampled the sandwich, then the soup, and let out a heavenly sigh.

"Wow...that's *good*. No Kraft cheese single slices in this, huh?" she teased.

"Only the best for you. I found a grocery store a few blocks away that has a good cheese selection."

Harper started to giggle, and Sef started to laugh himself. Her joy was infectious. "What?"

"I just can't picture you cheese shopping." She tried to take another bite but kept laughing, as did he.

"You're killing me." He had to stop her from laughing, or they would never eat.

"So Jessie betrayed the girl code." Harper shook her head, still smiling as she resumed eating.

"Girl code?" Sef wasn't sure what to make of that.

"Yeah, you know, girls have a code. You don't date each other's exes, and you don't tell boys stuff about your friend if it's secret. It's an honor thing."

"And Jessie broke this code of yours? Grilled cheese is a secret?"

"No, not really. I was kidding." She leaned back in her chair and finished the last of her sandwich before starting in on the soup.

He liked that she wasn't afraid to eat in front of him. A healthy appetite was a good thing. Females were never meant to eat low-calorie foods all the time, despite what Earth advertising said to the contrary.

"This is really nice," she said. Her eyes moved shyly to his face and then darted away again.

He gestured to the food. "Jessie said your parents liked to make this?"

"It was my mom's specialty. She had this old griddle, and she knew just how much to butter the bread, and she always used white bread. It's terrible for you, super processed, but it tastes amazing. She always knew when to make it for me or my brothers. And Dad would rope us into playing a board game after dinner. Even when Liam and Mason got older, they still played board games." She paused, and he swore he could feel her pain emanating from her. When she spoke again, her voice was softer and a little rough with emotion. "We haven't played any games in a long time." She seemed to brace herself for whatever she planned to say next, and he waited patiently.

"I think we've all closed off part of ourselves since K-Day," she said. "We all changed. Grief has a funny way of driving people together or wedging them apart. Losing Mom and Dad drove us apart. I know Liam and Mason are closer to each other, but that's because..." Her words trailed off into tense silence.

"Because?" He didn't expect her to answer, but he knew where she was going with this.

"Their hatred toward the Ks binds them together," she finally confessed.

"But not you?" He wondered how she'd respond to that.

"No. I don't hate the Ks. They aren't evil." That came as a relief. Sef took a sip of wine. "They're just bossy."

He almost choked. "Bossy?"

"Yeah. Sure, they *seem* nice and all, but they came here and started ordering us around, telling us it was for our own good. They don't share their tech, they tell us what to eat, tell us how to live...straight up bossy."

"But they let most humans, I mean, us, live our own lives."

That was mostly true. His people had only really controlled human activity when they'd stopped the meat industry, banned coal production, encouraged solar and wind power, and found safe ways to dispose of nuclear waste.

"But I hear things, you know? This talk of X-clubs. Outside the K Centers in the big cities."

"What do you know of these X-clubs?" He kept his tone mildly curious. He was well aware that humans had a distorted view of the clubs. Rumors grew legs quickly.

"Well, first off there's what you hear on the news. They're sex clubs where Krinar have sex with humans, and I heard they drink our blood too."

Sef restrained himself from licking his lips, remembering her blood on his tongue, how good she was. She didn't even remember that—she'd been too lost in pleasure. But she would someday, once she was his charl and he could talk to her honestly about it. He'd taken care not to drink too much, just enough to send her into a sexual high so she could relax and allow him to enter her without pain.

"I heard that sex with a K is intense," he said. He watched her take a large gulp of her wine. He feared he'd said too much because of the sudden gleam in her eyes.

"Sex with *you* is intense," she murmured, and her eyes flashed up so their gazes locked.

He nodded at her soup, hoping to distract her. "Finish your dinner." The last thing he needed was her figuring out he was an alien.

Harper grinned. She took two more spoonfuls and set her bowl aside.

"I thought perhaps we'd enjoy some wine by the fire." He put his dishes down and scooted his chair to align with hers so they touched end to end. She came closer, and it all felt too easy, too *right* to wrap one arm around her waist and pull her close to him. She shivered a little, and he reached up to wrap the blankets around them.

She snuggled into him and rested her head on his shoulder. He was quiet a long moment before pointing toward the sky.

"You see that constellation?"

"The Little Dipper?" Her hair tickled his throat in the faintest breeze. He could smell the sweet jasmine scent of her shampoo clinging to each strand like the lingering kiss of a delightful dream.

"Yes, that's the one." The Krinar had another name for it, the Flag Bearer, because it looked like an arm holding a flag. Of course, the star patterns looked different from Krina as compared to Earth, but he felt connected to Harper simply by looking upon the stars together. He nuzzled the crown of her hair before pressing his lips to it. "My mother loves that one more than the others." Holding her like this felt incredible. There was a soft, fuzzy feeling in his chest that he'd never experienced before. It was a little frightening, but he knew he wasn't sick. So what exactly was this strange emotion? For the first time in his long life, he wondered if he might be falling in love. If he was, it was a terrible and wonderful thing.

"Oh? Why's that?" She raised her head, pressing a soft kiss to his jaw that made his heart ache in a deep way that scared him.

"She says it looks like a ladle, which reminds her of feeding me and my brother when we were young because we had such huge appetites growing up."

"You have a brother? I didn't know that."

"We've only known each other for two days," he said with a chuckle. "But yes, I have a brother...Sam." He couldn't say the name Soren—*everyone* knew the ambassador by name. It would be too much of a risk.

"Older or younger?"

"We're twins, though I'm older by three minutes."

"Are you close?" Harper placed a hand on his chest just above his heart, and his heart beat faster in response.

"We were. Now, not so much. He was reckless when we were younger, always adventurous. He got lost for several months exploring a forest. We feared the worst. When we found him again, I was so relieved, but things had changed."

The full truth was that Soren had been exploring a distant world and had been captured by an alien race, and he'd been held hostage for three hundred years. When Soren had finally escaped and come home, he'd been quieter and yet angrier, a shadow of a long-endured pain in his eyes that haunted him still. And Sef had been helpless to save him or to heal him. Sef had become a guardian so that he could protect his people, especially from alien races.

"That's so sad," Harper said.

Sef smiled. "Things are better now, though not quite what they once were."

"You will find your way back to him. True bonds with siblings are unbreakable." Her fingers on his chest began to play with the fabric of his dark-blue button-up shirt. She unfastened the top two buttons and slid her fingers underneath to touch his skin.

That simple connection made him burn with desire, as well as something softer and sweeter than he'd ever felt in his life. Guilt ate at him about concealing who he really was, but there was no other way. He couldn't tell her because she would warn her brothers. He would do the same in her position. Family came first. Yet...now that he was going to claim Harper as his charl, he had this strange compulsion to put her first, even over his twin if it ever came to that. And that was the scariest thing of all. His brother's wild, irrational behavior toward his charl, Bianca, made so much more sense.

"Where do your parents live?" she asked. "Do you visit them often?"

"They live in Boulder. I don't get to see them as

often as I'd like." That was yet another lie. His parents were still on Krina, his home world. He hadn't been back there since the K-Day invasion of Earth.

"You shouldn't wait. I would give anything to see my parents again. You should visit them soon." She continued to stroke his chest, and he cradled her head as he gently claimed her mouth.

This woman was a drug to him, affecting him in a way no other had. He explored the shape of her mouth, and she parted her lips for him. Sef took his time kissing her, letting himself give in to every caress, every sweet side, every purr of pleasure as fully as he could as he cuddled her closer.

"Want to take this inside?" she asked when they took a moment to breathe.

"Why not beneath the stars?" He brushed his lips back and forth teasingly over hers after he suggested it.

"Someone might see us."

"None of the other buildings nearby are tall enough. You'll be safe from all but the cosmos above," he promised her.

She smiled and leaned over to straddle him. The blanket fell away as she rubbed herself against him. He groaned as he grew painfully hard beneath his jeans. She laughed softly as he hiked her dress up over her hips and ripped her panties off.

"You owe me some underwear," she teased.

"I suppose I do," he growled as he unzipped his jeans and shifted her over him.

They shared a look that was full of heat and hunger but also something more. Then he thrust into her welcoming heat. She was so small and tight, he couldn't imagine how he'd ever fit into her, now or the other times he'd been with her.

"*Ahh!*" she hissed, arching her back a little as she tried to take him deeper.

"Relax, Queenie," he breathed as he worked himself deeper inside her.

She did as he said and let gravity pull her down. He sank another few inches deeper, and they both shared a moan before he kissed her again. The whole experience was exciting, extending beyond their bodies. He held her hips tight, afraid to let go as she spiraled in ecstasy above him, building to a shattering climax. He followed her seconds later, a release so deep and satisfying that for the first time that he could remember his mind blanked. It simply cleared of all thoughts. It was the most peaceful thing he'd ever experienced. No worries, no strategies, no deceptions. He was himself, cocooned by tranquility. Harper collapsed against him, her body trembling.

"It's okay," he murmured. "It's okay."

He wasn't sure why he felt the need to reassure her. Perhaps he needed to reassure himself about the connection that continued to build between them. It took a long while for Sef to come back to himself. He was torn between a myriad of sensations in the aftermath of their pleasure. The weight of her body on his, the cool night air dancing upon his skin, the distant noise of King's Bar in full swing, and the ever-present press of time as he finally had to face reality.

He couldn't stay here with her forever, no matter how much he wanted to. This moment was one of stolen happiness, and it was all he would have with her before he had to leave, taking her brothers with him. And he'd lose her forever if she couldn't accept his true identity as a Krinar.

"Thank you, Seth," she whispered against his chest. "Thank you for helping me open up my heart again."

It was the only thing she could have said that could make him regret everything that was about to happen.

But he couldn't stop what had to be done.

8

———

Sef carried Harper back to her apartment and helped her change into her pajamas. She was so sleepy that she let him strip her naked and put her into her panties and an oversized T-shirt. Then he tucked her into bed and crawled in beside her. These might be the last few hours he would have to get to hold her before he betrayed her, the only female who had ever truly given him peace. If her brothers decided to act tonight, he would have to call in reinforcements, but it was far more likely that tonight's meeting would simply be that, just a meeting, in which case he could stay here a little longer before he had to reveal the truth to Harper.

Guilt knotted inside him, and his limbs quivered with flashes of anxiety. The only time he had felt this sick before had been when his brother had vanished off world. Three centuries he'd been told to believe his twin was dead when he was certain that he felt Soren's bond still linking them. It had been a torture he'd thought he would never experience again. Yet now he was caught in that same familiar grip of guilt and fear. He had something to lose now, something that meant more to him than his own life. When he took Harper's brothers into custody and revealed himself to be the enemy, she would hate him.

I have to protect my people. Her brothers are a threat to the peaceful relations we've worked so hard to establish between the Krinar and humans.

And it wasn't as if he could have another guardian make the capture either. He would still have to reveal himself at some point as being a Krinar. He couldn't live this human life forever, no matter how tempting Harper might be.

He lay awake, his eyes boring holes into the ceiling. An hour before the resistance meeting, he slipped out of Harper's bed and went up to his apartment. He notified Arus that he was going to monitor the resistance meeting.

At ten minutes until four a.m., the cameras picked up the King brothers allowing a number of men and women to enter the darkened bar and head toward the storeroom. Sef changed the view so he could see both the bar and storeroom interior, and he tuned in to their conversations.

"Thanks for coming on such short notice, every-one," Liam began. Mason stood behind him, arms folded across his chest, his expression somber like Liam's.

"We won't be discussing protests or social media awareness campaigns tonight. We have Mitch Davis here. He wishes to speak with you about an anti-K rally to be held outside the Kansas City K Center. Mitch, you have the floor."

A tall dark-haired man with hard brown eyes stood and faced the individuals seated in front of him.

"Since we want to keep this meeting short, I'll be brief. I have over a hundred volunteers who will be planting bombs on the walls of the Kansas City Center. We have a K on the inside who is sympathetic to our cause."

Mitch's words sent a bolt of fear through Sef. One of his own people was betraying them? The situation was far more serious than he had realized. Humans acting on their own posed little physical threat, but with access to their technology? The potential for disaster was all too real.

Mitch continued speaking. "The K has given us technology that can make our approach to the Center's walls invisible. We won't get caught. But we can't do it alone. We'll need people like you to be a distraction, carry signs, attract attention by making a scene. You were already planning a protest there, but we need you to step it up a notch. Make it a public rally, keep the Ks' focus on you so that we can do what we need to in order to bring down the walls of the Center. Then we will finally see what lies inside their fortresses and expose them to the world. We can make President Wells finally admit that the Ks are our enemies once we reveal them for what they really are."

The room seemed tense. People shifted uncomfortably as Mitch talked, but a few people looked eager to help. Sef studied Liam and Mason closely, since they were the leaders of this particular cell. Neither of them looked comfortable with the plan.

"Can you guarantee no one will be hurt by these bombs?" Liam asked.

"They should be small enough to break apart the walls, but not big enough to create damage that could reach residences or places of work," Mitch replied.

"But really, who cares if any Ks are in the way?" someone asked. Sef was sure he saw a smirk on Mitch's face when the question was asked.

"We've all seen what the Krinar are capable of," Liam reminded the men and women around him. "They can rip humans apart with their bare hands and can shake off gunshots like they're wearing body armor. Truth is, I'm not worried about hurting the Ks, because I'm not sure we can."

"Bullets are one thing—bombs are another," said the man from before.

"That may be," said Liam. "But humans are also going to be in the area, and we bleed a lot easier than they do. Bottom line, this shouldn't be about killing.

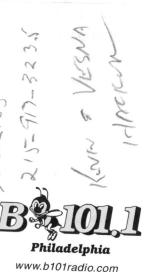

be about freedom. Exposing a K is a good idea, but we don't want loodshed of innocents, even if they am looked at Mitch. "If you can e killing anyone, including Ks, then

et for a long moment, just long ld detect he was about to lie. "Yes,

d Mason shared a glance, and they re. "We'll go over the details and 't want anyone here crossing lines they aren't comfortable with."

"Do what you have to, but don't take too long," said Mitch. "We have a narrow window of opportunity to work with here. Security routines that can change up, passcodes that can be changed. Once everything is in place, we'll need to move, with or without you."

"We'll meet here next week. Same time." Liam looked to Mitch, who nodded.

"I should know more from my K contact how to construct the bombs needed to break down the walls," Mitch added, a dark gleam in his eyes. This man was dangerous. Sef had seen that look before on a dozen worlds. Mitch was in it for the bloodshed, not because he believed in freedom. The cause was merely the justification for his baser instincts.

Sef continued to observe the meeting as the members went over more mundane matters and eventually dispersed into the night. Only Mason and Liam remained behind. Sef kept his focus on them and increased the volume. He recorded every word for evidence.

"Mason, I don't know about him. That guy creeped me out." Liam began to fold up the chairs and set them against one wall in the storeroom. "You remember Chris Hanson from high school?"

Mason nodded. "You thinking about his pit bull fighting ring?"

"Exactly. He told the judge he needed the money, but he enjoyed that shit way too much, you could tell."

"Yeah, I know where you're going. Fucker is creepy as hell, but we need him. Slogans, protests, and social media aren't cutting it. He's the only one I've met with a plan that might make a real difference. I don't like the idea of blowing up anything any more than you do. Too much room for error. But exposing the inside of a K Center? That's a game changer."

Mason helped his brother finish putting away the chairs, and the easy way they worked together in the small space without having to vocalize made Sef's heart twinge. Mason and Liam weren't unlike him and Soren. Familial bonds could run infinitely deep.

"Let's just look over the plan and have the vote," said Liam. "I don't want our friends going down with him if he turns out to be fucking batshit crazy. He could get us all killed 'for the cause.' I'd rather find a safer way to resist, but let's face it, with their advanced technology and refusal to even talk to us, they're not leaving us much choice."

"Either we stand up or we get stepped on," said Mason.

"Yeah, but remember, those who fight monsters..."

"...should take care not to become monsters." Mason finished Liam's sentence.

"Amen." Liam's solemn tone gave Sef hope that the man was speaking honestly. They weren't out to hurt the Ks, only to resist them, but how far were he and Mason willing to go?

Sef waited for the brothers to leave the storeroom, and then he sent Arus his report, stating that he might need a team the following week for the next meeting. Depending on how things went, he might have to raid the meeting there and then. Then he turned off his computer systems and headed to the roof to clear his head.

Once he was on the roof, he saw the chairs and the fire pit from his night with Harper, and he exhaled a slow, soft sigh of regret. He didn't want to lose her, not like this. It wasn't fair. She was his now, and he couldn't let her go, yet he would have to, because she couldn't possibly forgive him for what he had to do.

For the first time he truly understood how Soren must have felt when he'd faced losing his Bianca and why he had fought so hard to keep her.

We can't stay away. Our pull to them is simply too strong.

Sef cast his head back to stare at the infinite expanse of space. Many called space cold and dark, but all he saw were endless beacons of hope. New stars being born in stellar nurseries, planets forming along accretion disks in a slow but beautiful ballet of creation, galaxies spinning around one another, all of it pieced together by the beautiful enigma of what the humans called dark matter. They were close to discovering the secrets dark matter held, endless sources of energy and the delicate balance its presence in the universe provided. The Krinar had finally untangled its mysteries only a few millennia ago and were just now in the last thousand years applying it to their technology.

What would the humans do once they harnessed those secrets? Would they become an enlightened species like the Krinar, or would they destroy themselves? Ultimately, that was why they were here, to ensure the latter didn't happen. He knew without a doubt that if more men and women like Harper existed, then humanity could yet be saved.

And I want to do all I can to help them, he thought. An idea occurred to him, one that made his heart skip a beat. It was unlikely, perhaps even impossible...but it was the only way to save his little human female and possibly find a way to keep her.

————

HARPER COULDN'T SLEEP. SHE ROLLED OVER AND FOUND the bed empty. The clock on her nightstand flashed five thirty a.m.

Seth was gone?

"Seth?" Only silence greeted her. She climbed out of bed and pulled on some yoga pants and her house slippers before she left her apartment. She knocked on Seth's door, but no one answered. Her heart sank. Could he have left town already? Was it because she'd gotten too close?

"I'm such an idiot." She never should have opened her heart like that, let alone jumped his bones. She should have known better.

"Harper?" Seth's voice rumbled gently as he came down the stairs from the roof.

"Oh. I..." She blushed, glad the hallway was dim so he might not see it. "I woke up and you were gone, and I was afraid that..." Afraid that he didn't want her. The sentiment was left unspoken, but he seemed to read it on her face.

"You were afraid that I just fucked you and left you?" She nodded mutely as he joined her outside his door. He wrapped his arms around her waist and leaned in to nuzzle her cheek. "No chance. Come on, let's go back to bed." He helped her move back downstairs to her apartment.

"What were you doing up there?" she asked as she settled back in her bed. He stripped out of his clothes again so he could join her.

"Oh," he chuckled. "I was restless and wanted to just watch the stars for a bit before the sun came up. There's something about the night sky that soothes me."

"Me too."

He turned off the lights, and he climbed into bed with her. She clung to him as she let his body warm hers, trying not to admit to herself that she'd had a taste of what it would be like to lose him, even for just a moment. What would it feel like if he really left?

I'm insane. He's still a stranger, really. I shouldn't care that he might someday walk away. But I do. God help me, I do.

9

The week following that resistance meeting went by too fast for Sef. The blur of days had been fun as he'd helped Harper in the garage and then worked evenings at the bar. She and her brothers assumed he was desperate for money, but in truth he didn't want to waste a second of his time with her. Yet he couldn't ignore his mission to keep a close eye on Mason and Liam.

He couldn't deny the magic he felt working on cars beside Harper. Primitive as they were, there was something to be admired about the rudimentary mechanics involved and how they had evolved to incorporate more electronics in newer models. She was more than proficient at fixing them, of course. He'd only studied enough to make a good impression. Sometimes she would talk while she worked, offering bits of trivia she knew about whatever they were working on or interesting facts about engines in general. He loved the sound of her voice and the way her face lit up as she was engaged in something she enjoyed.

Now it was Saturday morning. He had just one more uncomplicated day with her, and all he could do was drink in the sight of her as she worked on an oil change. A small smudge of grease covered her chin, but she didn't seem to notice. Her muscled forearms gleamed with a sheen of sweat where she'd pushed her jumpsuit sleeves up. Sef was content to stand next to her, handing her tools as she worked and admiring the view of her animated face. Her long beautiful hair had been pulled back into a messy bun, and she wore a blue headband in the way human girls often did that made it look like a fashion statement. On her, it looked natural and adorable as hell.

"So I saw this one ship," Harper said as she studied the oil stick from the car before reinserting it. She'd been opening up about her thoughts on Krinar technology all morning.

"Yeah?" He found her insights interesting and sometimes amusing. There was only so much she could guess correctly based on observation alone, after all. But still, it was fascinating to hear her perspective on his kind without her knowing he was a Krinar.

"I saw it for just a brief minute on TV. Their ambassador was getting out of it. It was a small craft, one he landed on the White House lawn when he and President Wells were meeting for some kind of negotiations. Wow... I could see the inside of it, and he was in this chair, but then it morphed into a flat plank the second he stepped out. Then the ship door closed and I couldn't see anything else, but I want to know how they did it. What kind of technology do you think they're using to manipulate matter into shapes that quickly? Mimetic polyalloys?"

He could have told her that it involved a complex matter manipulation field integrated into a pliable conductive material. The best analogy he could make was being able to sculpt ice and then return it back to the same block of unchipped ice. Even if she could understand the science behind it, they were carefully guarded Krinar secrets.

"What would you do if you ever met a K?" he asked.

"Like for real? Like in person?" she asked, using her arm to try to wipe a fresh grease smudge off the tip of her nose.

He grabbed a nearby clean cloth and leaned forward to wipe it for her. "Yes, in real life. I mean, you seem to think they're...what did you call them? Bossy?"

Her gaze turned distant, so much that it seemed she was suddenly a thousand light years away from him. Then she gave her head a small shake and grinned. "I dunno. I'd probably shake his hand and say,

'Hey, pal, want to share a cheeseburger?'" She burst into a fit of giggles that had him laughing too.

"You'd want to create an international incident?" he teased. He could picture her doing exactly that, and all he could think of was her saying that to Soren and the look of horror that would be on his twin's face. He'd almost pay to see that happen.

"But seriously," she said, her face thoughtful again. "I don't know what I'd say. I guess I'd ask them, *Why us?* Why shove us aside just so they can live here? Surely there are a bunch of other planets they could take instead, right? Hell, you'd think they'd have terraforming tech and could just make their own."

Sef leaned against the car's side as she finished capping the oil. She removed the metal stand and lowered the hood so it clicked shut.

"Even if they did, terraforming takes time," Sef said cautiously. "I heard the Ks were searching for hundreds of thousands of years for planets, that they sent out the seeds of evolution to a number of places, waiting to see which planets would take Krina's genetic material the best. Rumor is this planet was one of the best."

"Ah, ripe for the harvest, huh? And we get the shaft." It was hard to miss the edge of her tone.

"Well, I dunno. If they wanted to get rid of us and move in, would any of us be left?" he asked. "You've seen what they can do, so I'd say the fact that they're mostly leaving us alone is a good sign. I guess that they really do want to share the planet with us. They like us...or so I've heard."

Harper wrinkled her nose. "*Like* us? How many towns like this have you come across in your travels, Seth? Towns clinging to life or they're already dead but don't know it yet? If they like us, they sure have a funny way of showing it."

Sef wished he could find a way to help her understand his people without giving away too much. "Think about how you would do it. Let's say you know you need a new planet to live on, and you have to take over one with a sapient species on it like us. How would you go about it while keeping panic and death to a minimum? The Ks took decisive control. Only a few of the more idiotic dictators and socialist leaders refused to cooperate, because those assholes don't care about the people in their countries. For them it's about keeping power for themselves. They didn't want to cooperate, and it cost them."

"I remember." Harper shuddered. Sef knew she would. Those unfortunate countries and their massive loss of life in the Great Panic that followed still haunted him. But his people hadn't been able to stop the violence that the humans had inflicted, mostly upon themselves.

"I guess it could have been way worse," she admitted. "With the Ks, I mean. They worked hard to make sure things went as smoothly as possible. They haven't taken over our government, at least so far as we know."

Sef shook his head. "Now you sound like a conspiracy theorist. The Ks don't need to control the government. If they wanted control of something, they'd just take it."

She huffed. "See, there you go again, reminding me why I don't like them."

He came up to her, gently trapping her from behind against the car she'd just finished working on. "*You* seem to like it when I take what I want," he reminded her in a low whisper, then nibbled her ear. Harper moaned and leaned back against him. Sef was glad Ruby, Jeff and Alan had all gone out for lunch and wouldn't be back for another forty minutes. They had the garage all to themselves.

"But you're not like a K. You're not...bossy." She struggled to try to speak as he cupped her breasts, kneading them and finding her nipples through her jumpsuit. Then he unzipped the suit so he could slide his hands inside to get to her thin tank top and bra.

"I'm not bossy?" he asked, nipping her shoulder as he started to peel her suit off her shoulders to free her arms.

"Well...maybe a little, but in a good way." She closed her eyes briefly.

"What's the bad way?" he asked, curious to know exactly what she meant.

"No, you're not...not like what I hear goes on at those Krinar X-clubs."

"Do you know what the X stands for?" he asked as he ground his pelvis against her, knowing she could fee his erection.

"What?" she murmured.

"Xenophile. Xeno-clubs are for K-obsessed humans." He waited, letting that sink in. "And you know what those Ks do there in these clubs to sweet little women like you?" He cupped one of her breasts, teasing it out of her bra as he pushed her tank top up and over her body.

"What?" she asked breathlessly and wriggled her ass, teasing him in a way that sent him spiraling into a wild, savage need to fuck her.

"Those big bad Ks take girls like you into rooms where the furniture floats off the ground. Then they pin them down and fuck them for hours." He managed to remove her bra, and her full bare breasts filled his hands.

"That's it?" she asked. He quickly spun her around and lifted her up onto the hood of the car so he could tug her jumpsuit down to her ankles. "I expected something more...kinky."

"That's only the beginning, or so I hear," he growled as he tried not to tear the suit. He was getting distracted and starting to realize he was letting on more than he should about the clubs.

"What else do they do?" She spread her legs wide as he stepped between her thighs.

He gripped her hips and jerked her farther down the hood so her hips were level with his and right at the edge of the car. Then he unzipped his jeans and pulled out his cock, stroking it with one hand as he gazed down at her. She was so fucking perfect, his sweet little Harper. So damn tempting with her full breasts and her curvy hips and that slit that was all wet for him. He rubbed against her, teasing her.

"Ks like to sink their teeth into a woman, drink her blood."

"So it's true," she said, though it seemed like she was only half listening. "Like a vampire."

"Not really. It's more like a drug, for both of them. They can get addicted to it. Crave it. Do anything to get it. And a K male is dominant—he won't let his woman escape him. He'll tie her down, handcuff her wrists, keep her in just the position he wants."

As he spoke, he gripped Harper's wrists in one of his hands and pinned them to the car hood just above her head. She gave a half-hearted attempt to break free, and when she couldn't, the sweet scent of her sensual hunger filled the air around them, drugging him almost as much as her blood.

"And then take her...like this." He thrust his cock inside her.

"Oh God, Seth," she whimpered as he sank into

her, giving her time to adjust. They'd made love all week—frantic, slow, rough, tender—and each time he'd tried to be careful when he first entered her.

"Don't go slow," she panted. "Want...fast."

He drew in a breath, marveling at how perfect this human female was. He gave her what she wanted and slammed home, balls-deep inside her. She hissed as he withdrew, and he rammed in again. He possessed her hard and fast as they mated in a frenzy. His mind and body hummed with thoughts of how it would feel to taste her again, but he resisted the urge. He had to be careful. He couldn't send her into an overload, not in the middle of the day like he had that very first time.

Despite his best intentions, he sank his teeth into her shoulder, holding her still, but he didn't break the skin. He just pounded into her over and over. Even when he felt her body tense and she cried out as she climaxed, he didn't stop, *couldn't* stop. Part of him knew this might be the last time, that this might be his final taste of her lips, the smell of her skin and the warmth of her channel wrapped around his shaft.

Harper moaned, going limp beneath him, and he felt that primal thrill he always got knowing he'd fucked her into languid ecstasy. Their gazes met as he continued to jackknife his hips against her body.

"Seth...I think...I think I'm falling in love with you," she whispered.

The words obliterated all rational thought from

him. He emptied himself into her, their bodies still fused, heat singeing where they touched as he tried to catch his breath and process what she'd said.

Her lashes fanned down, and she turned her face away. "Don't say anything. I just...I wanted to tell you. I don't expect anything. It simply felt right to say it." She bit her bottom lip, so shy and vulnerable at this moment that it made him ache.

Lowering his head, he stole her lips in a tender kiss different from the lovemaking they'd just shared. He told her in his own way that he might be falling in love with her too, that she could have been his charl in another life, been the companion of his heart forever, if only he didn't have to break hers.

After a moment they disentangled themselves, and Harper got dressed. She wrinkled her nose as she heard the auto shop front door open.

"Damn. Ruby's back. I'd better go clean up. Since I'm done for the day and Alan and Jeff can finish the rest, do you want to...hang out before your shift tonight?"

Sef gave her that bad-boy grin he knew made her wet for him. "You bet. I'll let Ruby know, and then we'll spend the afternoon together."

The smile she gave him made him feel like a damned god. If only...if only he felt he deserved it.

10

The afternoon sun soaked into Harper's skin as she lay in the bed of Mason's pickup truck. She'd borrowed it for the afternoon and was enjoying just lying in the back with a thick picnic blanket beneath her and Seth by her side.

"Do you ever think about what things would be like if the Ks hadn't come?" she asked him.

He lay flat on his back, her head resting against one of his biceps. "Sometimes," he answered, but didn't elaborate. "You?"

"Yeah, a lot." She closed her eyes, letting the sunshine turn the backs of her eyelids gold.

"Because of your parents?"

"Not just them. Sometimes I wish I lived in a big city near a K Center. I'd like to see their technology up close. Just to get a sense of things, you know?"

"You really are curious about them, aren't you?" Seth's laugh was gentle rather than mocking. After their explosive sex in the shop, she'd realized he knew more about the Ks than he'd let on before. He must have learned about them during his travels, or maybe he was just spreading rumors he'd heard as if they were gospel truth.

"I can't help but be curious."

"Curiosity is good. The most creative people in the world are full of curiosity."

"I'm not creative," she said.

"Sure you are."

She shrugged. "Even if I am, I can't be creative enough when I—"

"When what?"

"When...I get the headaches." She couldn't believe she was going to admit this to him. "I have dyslexia." She waited for the questions, or for him to withdraw from her.

"A tough condition. It must cause you a lot of difficulty."

Here we go, she thought. *He's going to finally see me for my useless self and walk away.*

"You're an incredible woman. I can't imagine how strong you must be to handle the headaches and the trouble reading and writing. It makes me proud to know you, proud to be with you."

Oh God, she hadn't expected him to say *that.*

"You mean it?" She hated how needy she sounded. Xander had always pitied her, as if staying with her had been a sacrifice on his part.

Seth leaned over her, kissing her slow and sweet in a way that made her heart shiver with secret longing for things she shouldn't want, like a life with him. "I mean it, Queenie. You're fucking amazing."

She sighed as she looked toward the horizon. The sun was starting to drop.

"We should head back," Seth said, disappointment heavy in his tone.

"Yeah, you've got the late shift at the bar." She would probably spend all night in the bar finding excuses to help him because she couldn't get enough of this man. She was officially addicted to Seth. They packed up the blanket and headed back into town.

Mason met them outside the auto shop. He'd figured out this past week, along with Liam, that she was seeing Seth, but they'd taken it fairly well.

"You kids have a nice day out?" Mason teased her.

Harper tossed him back his truck keys. "Yes, as a matter of fact, we did."

Seth smiled and waved her on inside. "I'll be with you in a minute."

It was clear Mason wanted to talk to him and that she wasn't supposed to stick around. So she rushed upstairs to freshen up. But as she thought back to Seth's face, she'd seen something in his eyes that left her worried. He seemed...distant now that they were back at the shop. Distant and regretful. It had been just a flash in his eyes, but she hadn't missed it, and that scared her. It felt...like goodbye.

———

"So...," Mason drawled as they watched Harper leave.

"So...," Sef echoed carefully.

"You and Harper, huh?"

"Yeah." He was careful not to say too much. He knew Liam and Mason were aware of his romantic relationship with their little sister, and the last thing he wanted was to upset them.

"She dated this real dick named Xander a few years back. Did she tell you?" Mason asked as they headed to the bar.

"No, she didn't." The fact that she hadn't told him about this other man bothered him. Did she still have feelings for him? Did she still want to be with him? Unlikely, given how Mason had just described him.

"Well, he was a grade A douchebag, man. Grade A. Cheated on her the night of their anniversary." Mason snorted at the memory. "He was a pretty boy, like you."

"I'm not a pretty boy," Sef replied, bristling a little. Mason and Liam were attractive as well, and he was attempted to call Mason the insult right back.

"Pretty, handsome, whatever. You got looks, and you know it. Point is, she's not going to get her heart broken again. Now, I can see this shit is serious already. So if you read the signals wrong, if you thought this was casual and were still planning to leave at some point, you need to leave tonight. Or else you stick around until she decides to end things. You get what I'm saying?"

Sef didn't speak for a moment, considering what Mason was really saying. Finally he nodded, and lied right to his face. "I'm sticking around."

"Good. Glad to hear it. Liam and I think you're an okay guy. Don't make us regret thinking that."

Sef just nodded again as they entered the bar to start their shift for the evening. It was going to be a long night, and then he had to wait for the resistance meeting, and after that...well, he refused to think about what tomorrow would bring.

When the bar closed up for the night, Sef headed to Harper's apartment to join her in bed for a few hours. He curled up around her, and she sighed his name in a dreamy way before falling back to sleep. He lay there, holding her, watching the digital clock on her nightstand tick down the hours.

At a quarter to four, he left her and headed back to his apartment, quickly setting up his surveillance net and scanning the day's footage for anything of importance. Arus had left a message to inform him that the team was in place, waiting for his signal.

He could see Liam and Mason now, ushering people inside the bar toward the storeroom. Mitch was among them.

As soon as the meeting started, Sef transferred the visuals to a small handheld device. Then he crept down to the garage and waited in the hall that connected to the bar.

"Okay, everyone, settle down. I know we all voted yesterday via text message to help Mitch." Liam caught the attention of those gathered. "Mitch met with the K sympathizer, and we've set a date for three days from now. I know that's not a lot of time, but we can't afford to wait."

"Right," Mitch cut in. "My connection said that he can only get us the bombs tomorrow, and we have to use them within a few days or else someone will notice them missing from the armory."

"And you're sure we won't hurt anyone?" Liam said. "We only agreed to this based on that promise."

"Yes," Mitch sighed. "No one gets hurt. Jesus, for fuck's sake, you know the plan. Nobody will be near the explosions. Let's just do this, okay?"

Sef tensed, muscles rigid with apprehension. Tonight was the night. They had to capture the rebels before they got ahold of any Krinar weapons.

He tapped the hidden comm piece in his ear. "Team one, stand by. Wait for my signal."

"Confirmed," one of the guardians replied.

"All right. Since we're all so concerned, let's go over the plan, then," Mason said. "Point one: Where's the safest place to put the bombs?" He pointed toward a layout of the Kansas City K Center on a large piece of paper that he'd spread out on a table. Mitch and Liam and the other rebels leaned over it to get a better look. "Now, this is what we believe will provide the best exposure once the dust settles. We've looked over traffic patterns to know when it's not in use, so this is where the first batch will go..."

It was all Sef needed. He spoke quickly. "Engage. Subdue at all costs, but do not kill. Stunners only. I will meet you inside once we have everyone secured."

"Yes, Commander," one of the guardians replied.

Sef shut down the screen and tucked it into his pocket. Then he slipped into Harper's office to wait until it was all over.

———

THE SOUND OF AN EXPLOSION COMING FROM THE BAR woke Harper with a jolt. Fire sirens blared, and she winced, covering her ears.

What the hell? Was it a gas explosion? One of the cars in the shop?

She grabbed her keys and hurried into the garage. It was dark and quiet, which meant whatever had happened had to be in the bar.

Harper threw open the door to the bar, and flashes of blue light burst across her vision. Tall men in white uniforms were aiming small objects that looked like laser pointers at the men and women trying to escape. Her brothers dove behind the bar, grabbing their shotguns, which Harper knew they kept loaded with rock salt rather than bullets. They didn't like hurting people, but now they were desperately trying to return fire on the men in white.

But these weren't men. They were Ks. The Krinar were here, shooting at her brothers. Their resistance cell must have been discovered.

Oh God, oh God, oh God...

They were going to get themselves killed!

"Mason, Liam!" She tried to step into the bar area, but someone grabbed her and pulled her back into the hall. A hand covered her mouth.

"Hush. It's not safe. Stay here." Seth's comforting voice made her relax, but only a little. Tears stung her eyes as she saw Liam trying to shelter one of the women, and a blue bolt struck his chest. He crumpled to the floor. The woman tried to pull him back behind the bar, but she was hit too and went down. Mason roared, opening fire on the Ks before he was clipped in the shoulder by blue light and fell.

Harper watched the nightmare unfold in slow motion, until finally everything was quiet and horribly still. Her head was still swimming as Seth gently released her.

"Stay put," he growled. "It's not safe." She nodded numbly as he walked into the bar. It took a moment for what he was doing to sink in. She tried to warn him to come back, but the words turned to ash upon her tongue as he stepped up to one of the Krinar and shook his hand.

"No..." Seth had sold her brothers out to the Krinar. He had betrayed them and gotten them killed.

A fissure cracked deep within her fragile heart. The pain was so great that she couldn't breathe. She sank to her knees, leaning against the wall for support.

The Krinar agents began placing metal cuffs on the bodies and carrying them outside. When a Krinar male went to grab Mason, she lunged out of the hall, screaming at the alien to let her brother go. She skidded to a stop as Seth moved to block her from the Krinar, who were now aiming their weapons at her.

"Commander?" one of the Krinar asked.

Commander? She glanced around with dawning horror as she realized that he hadn't just betrayed them to the Krinar—he was one of them.

"Stand down. She is mine. She is not a resistance fighter," Seth announced.

One of the Krinar spoke quickly to Seth in their

own language, and he replied in the Krinar tongue. She heard the word *charl* and shivered. She'd heard that word before. It meant *slave*. There had been rumors for years about charls being sex slaves for the Krinar.

"You're one of them," she said, her tone full of venom. He had used her—used her, betrayed her, and killed her family.

"I am," Seth confirmed.

"You killed my brothers!" A black fury rose up within her on sulfurous wings, clawing its way out of her as she screamed in rage and pain. She was going to kill him. She balled her fist and swung, but she was no match for Seth. He caught her fist mid-swing without even trying.

"Stop it, you little fool. They aren't dead," Seth snapped, catching her by the waist and lifting her up. She kicked and thrashed, her slippers flying off. She tried to sink her teeth into his arm, but she couldn't bend far enough to reach him. One of the Krinar males spoke up.

"Are you sure she's yours, Commander?"

"Yes." Seth suddenly jabbed a small device into her arm, but she didn't get a good look at it.

"What did you do to me? What did you..." Everything turned fuzzy. She slumped in his arms as her legs gave out, but she was still conscious.

"Calm down, Harper. Breathe. Your brothers are

alive. We only stunned them. Nod if you understand." Harper managed a weak nod. "Good. Your brothers are being detained for anti-K and terrorist activities. They will be questioned, and their memories will be erased. They—"

She shook her head. "No, please, Seth," she begged. "Don't take them from me. I'll do anything. I..."

He stared at her a moment longer. "Anything?"

"Yes. Anything." She struggled to keep her eyes open, but everything was going dark.

"Promise to be mine forever. And I will guarantee their safety and their memories."

Be his? Belong to the man who had lied to her, used her, and broken her heart? Forever? But she had to say yes. Mason and Liam were the only family she had left, and she loved them. She would do anything for them. Even sell her soul to a Krinar bastard.

"Yes," she said.

"Put those two on a separate transport vehicle." Seth spoke to the Krinar agents who were lifting up Liam and Mason's limp bodies. "Take them to the Kansas City Center, and I will see to them." Seth looked down at her and gave a soft triumphant smile.

"I will make you a very happy charl, I promise." He kissed her, but all she could feel were her tears and the fissure in her heart tearing even wider as she finally slipped into unconsciousness in the arms of her enemy.

———

Sef scooped Harper's body up in his arms.

"What do you wish to do with the King brothers?" Trevlin, one of the guardians, asked. "Do your orders still stand?" Clearly the man thought he'd just said that to comfort the human woman.

"Yes. I want to deal with them personally. My surveillance shows that they wanted no bloodshed of our people. That may well save them from having their memories wiped, but they will need to be rehabilitated. Keeping Harper as my charl will go a long way for their compliance."

Trevlin smirked. "So you wish to use her to keep them in line, and use them to keep her as your charl?"

"Exactly." He knew his little human would be furious when she woke up. Furious, afraid, and hurting because he'd betrayed her and lied to her. Now he just needed to find a way to convince her that he cared about her and that there would be no more lies between them.

Trevlin confirmed something with a subordinate and faced Sef. "The ship is ready. Any other orders?"

"Yes, close the bar and the auto shop for now. Contact the woman employed by the garage named Ruby. She is to be given control over the bar and the shop until I decide what to do with them. Station a guardian in the region to watch over the businesses and residences clandestinely until we are sure they are safe. Also, clean out the apartment on the first floor. Have everything inside packed up and sent to my residence at the Kansas City Center. My charl will need her belongings and clothing to help her feel comfortable."

He started to leave the bar but paused to give Trevlin one more order. "You will find some blueprints in the main desk of the auto shop. Pack those as well." Then he carried Harper to the waiting transport ship. A number of humans had gathered a little distance away to watch what was going on, but no one dared to stop them from taking their prisoners on board.

Sef held Harper close to his chest as he headed for a small set of living quarters inside the transport. The ship was designed for planetary travel only, but it did have a bedroom and a bathroom. He carried Harper inside and pulled back the covers on the bed before laying her down. He tucked her in and left her locked securely in the cabin. The sedative he had given her would last for a few hours. Long enough for him to get her settled at his residence in the Center. The challenge of winning her trust back would begin, and he knew it was going to be a tough battle.

11

————

Harper came awake slowly, as though caught in the thin, glittering fabric of a deep and hauntingly beautiful dream. She had lain in Seth's arms as they had spoken of the stars and the secrets they held for their futures. Seth had seen her for who she was, as both a woman and an inventor. She wasn't broken; she wasn't damaged. With him, she was just herself.

She stirred, and the tendrils of the dream fell away. She stared in confusion at the room around her. She was in a bedroom, lying on a large bed, the fluffy white comforter a gentle contrast to the robin's-egg-blue walls. She peeled the comforter away and saw she was still in her pajamas. Pain flared in her skull, no doubt a reaction to the sedative Seth had given her, and she whimpered as everything came rushing back.

The fight, the arrests, the betrayal, the aliens taking

her brothers away, her begging for Seth's mercy, agreeing to be his charl, *his slave*, to keep her brothers from having their memories erased.

"What have I done?" Her voice broke as she covered her face with her hands.

She remained in bed awhile longer, letting her panic and grief subside before she ventured out of the room. They sure as hell weren't in Lawrence anymore, but she had no idea where they were. The window in the bedroom had been sealed shut, and she thought it wise not to break it. But through it she saw only dense trees that blocked her line of sight from anything farther than twenty yards.

As she explored her surroundings, she realized she was in a small but comfortable-sized house of two floors. The bedroom she'd woken up in was upstairs. There were three other rooms—one guest bedroom, an office, and a large bathroom. Downstairs she found the kitchen, the dining room, and a cozy living room with a large monitor. Everything was sleek in design and modern with a soft neutral palette of white, beige, and a pale frosty blue.

And it was all empty. There was no one else around. She'd found the front door locked as well as the downstairs windows. She still couldn't see anything outside except a lovely garden and trees. She padded barefoot onto the kitchen tile as she continued to look around. She licked her lips, desperate for a glass of water.

"Hello?" she called out, half hoping Seth would answer and half hoping she would never see the traitorous asshole ever again.

A soft, lilting female voice echoed all around her. "Hello. How may I help you?"

Harper leaped nearly a foot in the air before she realized no one was actually there. Which meant it had to be the house. The Krinar version of Alexa, perhaps?

"Um...I would like a glass of water, please." She crossed her arms over her middle, her gaze sweeping around the kitchen nervously. There was a sink but no faucet and no glasses that she could find in any cabinets.

"Certainly," the voice replied.

A second later a panel on the wall opened, and a tall blue glass full of water was visible on a shelf. Harper took the glass and marveled at how the wall panel closed itself back up without leaving a trace of having been there.

She reached out and ran her fingertips along the wall, using her nails to try to find even the slightest seam where the panel had to be, but she found nothing.

"I'll be damned." She would love to know how they did that.

"I'm sorry, can you please repeat your request?" the voice asked.

"Oh, it was nothing," Harper said, and then she spoke again. "Hey, what should I call you?"

"I have no name designation," the voice said politely.

Well, Alexa and Siri were too cliché. "Um... How about Linda? You sound like a Linda to me."

"I will respond to Linda if you wish."

Harper grinned. This was kind of fun. "Excellent. Okay, Linda, where am I?" She felt like she was playing twenty questions with a robot.

"You are in the Krinar Center just north of Kansas City in the United States of America, planet Earth, system Sol—"

"Got it. Thanks, Linda." She didn't need Linda giving her the full universe address. She finished her glass of water and pondered what else she could ask.

"Who owns this place?" She hopped up onto the kitchen island and waited.

"This unit is currently occupied by Commander Sef."

Go figure. Advanced alien computer technology and this one had a lisp. "I think you mean Seth. How do you spell it?"

"His name is spelled *S-e-f*. Commander Sef is a leading guardian of the Krinar people. His brother is

Ambassador Soren. Sef is the son of Sarina and Sarket."

"Holy shit, his brother is the ambassador?" How had she not seen the resemblance before now? She felt stupid...but Soren had dark hair and dark eyes, not like Sef.

"That is correct." Linda's voice continued to echo through the kitchen.

Harper leaped off the kitchen island and headed for the front door again. She was done. She wasn't sticking around.

"Linda, be a dear and unlock the front door, please."

"I'm sorry. My orders are to keep you confined to the house."

"Who gave you those orders?"

"Commander Sef. I follow all orders he provides."

"I'll bet you do," Harper growled. "Linda, where's your control box?" Harper wasn't completely useless with computers. The coding made her head hurt, but the basic engineering of a system was well within her talents. Of course, this was Krinar tech, so...

"I have no control box."

That answer deflated Harper's hopes, but she wasn't out of options. "Do you have any kind of system settings that I could adjust?"

"My systems are controlled remotely by

Commander Sef. Should I message him your concerns?"

"No! Definitely don't do that. Just let me think a minute." She began to pace around the living room. Thankfully, Linda remained silent.

"Linda, where is Sef right now?"

"His location has been designated as classified."

Great, just great. "When will he be back?"

"Approximately three minutes. I alerted him the moment you woke up, as per his instructions."

Harper stilled. "Linda, if you were an actual person, I would punch you in the face."

Linda did not respond, which was probably a good thing. If she got into an argument with someone who wasn't even real, she would need some serious therapy. Harper checked every possible exit again, and when those possibilities were exhausted, she tried throwing a chair at the large window facing the living room. It didn't even scratch the glass.

"Shit!" Harper flung herself onto the couch, hating how soft and comfortable it turned out to be.

A few minutes later, right on schedule, the door to the residence opened. Harper stared at the man in the doorway in confusion. Who was he? She recognized him, and yet she didn't.

He was dark-haired now, not blond, and the sunlight behind him hinted at lighter russet tones in his hair. And his eyes... Gone were the endless depths of stormy blue. Now they were dark-brown irises that swirled with a subtle golden hue. But his face was the same, the strong chin, hard jaw, and that damnable sensuous mouth.

"Harper." He said her name softly, though it now lacked the slight midwestern accent of her sweet, seductive drifter. Her imposter. Her heart tightened in pain. She stared at him from the couch for a long minute.

"Was any of it real?" she asked. "Was anything you told me true?"

Sef closed the door. She kept her eyes glued to his movements to see if there was a trick to opening it, but she didn't see anything aside from a slight flick of his hand above the knob. Then he walked around the couch and sat down beside her. She shrank away, needing to keep her distance. This man was a stranger, after all. And dangerous.

"Much of it was true," he admitted, then reached for her leg as though to touch her knee. She jerked away, and he pulled his hand back in response.

"What was true, exactly?" she demanded, but her tone was softer, her throat still tight with pain.

"My feelings for you," he said.

Harper scoffed.

"Yes, well...I was truthful about my brother and parents, though I had to alter the specifics." He dragged his fingers through his hair as though trying to decide how to talk to her.

"It isn't enough," she countered. "Too much of who you claimed to be was a lie, right down to your looks. I trusted you! You took advantage of that trust, and you used me, didn't you?"

He didn't argue with her, didn't insist that what was between them had nothing to do with Mason and Liam.

"Harper...I'm sorry. I didn't... You weren't part of the plan."

"And that makes everything okay, huh?" She curled her arms around her knees as she drew them up to her chest. They were silent a long, uncomfortable moment before she spoke again.

"I want to see my brothers."

Something flashed in Sef's dark eyes, but she couldn't read it. "You will when you have accepted your place as my charl."

"Can't wait to play with your human toy?" she shot back.

"No," he growled. "I need to be sure of your obedience to me to keep you safe. It's clear that not even our own Centers are safe from resistance fighters. I don't want harm to befall you. Once you trust me, you'll have your freedom again."

"I don't believe you, and I sure as hell don't trust you."

He glared at her. "I don't care what you believe. I speak the truth, Harper." He rose from the couch and addressed the room.

"Please prepare two salads and namiba juice."

Linda replied, "Of course, Commander Sef."

He entered the kitchen and a moment later removed two plates and two glasses from the wall.

Harper watched closely to see if he did anything special or different than she had in the kitchen earlier. "How does she do that?"

"I am not able to discuss our technology with you. Only charls trusted by their cheren are allowed to know such things."

"Well, I guess I'll never know," she said, staring hard at him. "Because I fucking hate you."

"No, you don't. You have an affection for me. That hasn't changed. Now come and eat your lunch. You slept for seven hours, and I know you're hungry."

She really was hungry but it didn't matter that her stomach was rumbling or how good food really sounded right then. She was too pissed off to give him the satisfaction.

"Harper, you will eat, or I will do something you will not like."

"If you are looking for a willing pet, threats of violence are just going to make me hate you more."

He arched one brow. "Oh, I had no intention of being violent. I intend to take you to my bed and remind you how much you *do* like me. Those are your two options. Eat, or be taken my bed."

They shared a look, hers full of rage, his one of firm determination. He wanted to take her to bed and remind her how much she liked it when they fucked? *Damn him!* She wanted to scream at his quietly arrogant demeanor.

If she had something sharp or heavy nearby, she would've grabbed it and thrown it at him. Unfortunately, the only thing near her was a pillow. She punched the pillow once before stalking over to the dining room table as he set a salad bowl down in front of her.

"Can't a girl get a decent burger around here?" she asked. It was nice to take a potshot at his people's veganism. Unfortunately, her words didn't seem to faze him.

"We have excellent meat substitutes that you would never be able to distinguish from the real thing, but try the salad first. I think you'll like it."

He took the chair opposite hers, neither of them speaking as they ate. And she hated to admit it, but the salad was good. She reached for the glass of juice and took a hesitant sip. It was amazing, like cranberry juice with hints of lemon and cinnamon.

"What did you call this again?" she asked, unable to deny her curiosity.

His brows rose, but he didn't look displeased. "That's namiba juice. It's a little like your apples in shape and size, but it grows into a blue fruit when it's ripe. We've been growing several of our native fruits and vegetables in our Centers here, testing in controlled batches to determine if they will be invasive or not. Earth's soil composition is not too different from Krina, and we are able to keep some of our more vulnerable flora from going extinct now."

"Extinct? What do you mean?"

Sef hesitated, and Harper studied his face, searching for any trace of the man she'd started to fall in love with. "Soon life on our planet will be unsustainable. Krina's star is far older than your sun, and it is dying. We have time still, and our people are good at thinking and planning ahead. Eons ago, we sent the seeds of evolution out into the galaxy, into what you call 'Goldilocks Zones' where life could potentially survive. Your planet took well to our genetic material, and when what you call hominids began to develop, we adjusted your evolution further. In some ways, you are like distant cousins to us. As a result, you are biologically compatible with us—not for procreation at the moment, but certainly for sex." His gaze swept over her, and despite her best efforts, her body flared to life as she remembered all too well how compatible they were.

She cleared her throat and focused on their discussion. "Were there other planets that responded like ours?"

Sef shook his head. "There have been other planets with habitable environments, but the life existing there is either incompatible or not friendly or developed enough. Like Zaruth."

He took another bite, and she did the same. When he didn't go on to explain what Zaruth was, she pressed him on it.

"Okay, I'll bite. What's Zaruth?"

"It's a planet my brother, Soren, explored. Long before we came here, Soren was an explorer for our people. He journeyed to planets in other systems that had been seeded long ago, conducting progress reports and looking for evolved races with potential or that required further biocompatibility adjustments. But during his expedition to Zaruth, he was captured by the humanoids who live there. He was kept prisoner for more than three hundred years in the most unimaginable conditions. We didn't know the depth of what had happened to him until he came home. My parents held out hope he was alive for about fifty years. I..." His voice grew rough. "I never gave up, even when everyone told me to. I could tell he was still alive."

She saw the ghost of that pain lingering in those golden-brown eyes, which she understood all too well.

After her parents' car had been found and only her father's body was pulled from the car, she had prayed that her mother had survived, but that was impossible. Still, she'd believed deep inside that she was alive somehow. But as the years had passed, Harper had finally been forced to accept that her mother's body had simply washed away.

"So what you said about Soren, that was true?"

"After a fashion. Centuries instead of months and another planet instead of a forest. But essentially true."

"And you really are twins?"

"Yes. It's very rare on Krina, far more so than with humans. And are were natural twins. Since the development of nanocytes increased our lifespan exponentially, our birth rate declined to prevent overpopulation. Today births are rare, and most Krinar females do not naturally conceive—their children are carefully planned genetically to ensure good health. My brother and I were a happy accident for our parents."

Harper sensed where he was headed. "So you and Soren have a deep connection, the whole twin thing people always talk about?"

He nodded. "We can sense each other most of the time. General feelings, anyway."

"So for three centuries you sensed he was alive, and no one believed you?" As much as she didn't like Sef or what he had done to her brothers, she did feel sympathy for him. To lose someone that close to him for so long and still know he was alive while everyone else said he had to be dead? She couldn't imagine the pain.

"I never gave up believing he was alive, but I finally resigned myself to never seeing him again. It's why I changed my duties. I wasn't always a guardian."

"What is a guardian?" She didn't want to interrupt him, but she had a thousand questions. "Some kind of cop?"

"It's somewhere between your policeman and your FBI. We enforce our laws and protect our people."

"Oh..." So he was a Krinar cop. She tried to imagine him wearing aviator sunglasses and eating doughnuts. The thought almost made her giggle, but he was the farthest thing from that. He was more like the sexy lead detectives on TV shows. The ones who wore button-up shirts with their sleeves rolled up, their hair tousled as they spent late nights solving murders and slipping exhausted into the beds of beautiful women.

"What did you do before? I mean, before you were a guardian?"

His lips curved in a rueful smile. "An engineer, believe it or not. I designed some of our earlier technology." He watched her, and she had a feeling he was waiting for her to react. She didn't, so he continued. "I saw the blueprints in Ruby's desk. The ones you drew."

"It's not like they'd work," she said, her tone quiet, and she looked away from him. "I was just noodling around, trying to see if I could understand the fundamentals."

Sef moved fast, coming around the table to sit beside her. He caught her chin in his hand, gently forcing her to face him.

"You're closer than you realize. Keep working on them. I'm having them brought here, along with all of your belongings. They will be delivered this evening. Now, you may decorate this home as you like while I am away. The central core system can—"

"Sorry, the what?"

"The computer that operates the house."

"Oh, gotcha. You mean Linda."

"Yes?" the house trilled in response to her name being spoken.

Sef quirked an eyebrow at that. "You gave it a name?"

"Why not? Seems a bit stuffy to just call it 'computer.'"

Sef had no way to reply to that, so he didn't. "The central core system can prepare more than just food. It can provide you with almost anything you desire. I wish for you to be happy here."

She almost pitied him, thinking he could win her over under duress. But part of her wanted to believe him, to trust the sincerity in his eyes. The problem was he was a masterful liar. He couldn't be trusted. So she would lie right back. She would earn his trust, and then she'd escape and find a way to free her brothers. They would get the hell out of here and go into hiding. Like the slogan said on some of those biker jackets: *Live Free or Die.*

But she would have to be careful not to concede to him too easily. He wouldn't trust a sudden change of heart.

"I will never be happy here, not as a prisoner." She nodded toward the front door.

"You aren't a prisoner, but I did not want you leaving until we had a chance to talk. We have high security, and if you ran, the other guardians might have taken you to a detention center."

"Is that where they would torture me?" she asked coldly.

He sighed. "No, we don't torture humans, but if they felt you were a threat, you would have had your personality adjusted. I don't want that to ever happen to you."

"You don't want a compliant sex slave? Wouldn't that make things so much easier for you? Just melt my brain and pop in a brainless sex toy program." Pain choked her into further silence.

Sef sighed heavily and bowed his head. She'd hit a nerve with that. "No, that's the last thing I want. I like you exactly as you are, even hating me as you do now. My feelings for you are true." He cupped her face in both his hands and moved in to kiss her.

It took every ounce of her self-control not to rear back. She wanted to scream, to hit him over the head with a vase or a fridge, but the second his lips touched hers, she felt the awakening of that tender passion he'd shown her before. His breath quickened as her body gave in to his kiss.

It all came back—the delicious hunger, desperate desire, and the knowledge that if she let him, he would strip her bare and take right then and there.

"No..." She pushed away, and he let her. Their breath mingled as they remained close enough for her to feel his heat.

"Harper," he growled. "Don't fight your attraction. I know you want me."

"Don't you get it? I wanted *Seth*. I don't know *you* at all." She rushed from the dining room up the stairs and threw herself onto the bed.

"Harper," Linda's voice chimed. "I sense you are in distress. What can I do to help?"

She buried her face in the pillows. "Nothing. Get lost."

A few minutes later, Sef stood in the doorway of the bedroom.

"I must return to work. If you need to talk to me, use the house's voice command."

"You mean Linda?" If she could find a way to annoy him, she was going to use it.

"Yes, Linda if you wish. She can summon me at any

time. I'll be back this evening to show you the Center, if you like." He hesitated. "*If* you behave while we are out, I can arrange for a visit to see your brothers tomorrow."

Hope blossomed in her chest. That was worth putting up with him for a while. "Really?" Knowing where they were and what conditions they were being kept in was vital. If she was going to escape with them, she would need information.

And she would need trust.

12

Sef stared at the monitors inside his office in guardian headquarters. He'd spent the last hour watching the private security feed to his residence, keeping an eye on Harper. The way they'd left things— her crying, him feeling like a villain—the entire situation had left a raw, bitter taste in his mouth. So he'd decided to check on her and ended up suffering right along with her.

Harper hadn't moved from his bed. She just lay there, crying into her pillow. The sight of her in such pain was tearing him apart. He would rather have faced a hundred resistance fighters armed to the teeth with Krinar weaponry than see her like this.

But what else could he do? He had his duty, and protocol had to be observed. He couldn't just let her roam free in the Center until he was certain she wouldn't do anything. His people wouldn't hurt her, but if something happened, she might make the other guardians nervous. They could stun her and detain her and even erase her recent memories before he was notified. He could change that—or rather, she could. If he officially claimed her as his charl, she would have that protection. But he wouldn't—no, *couldn't*—do that until he knew she wanted it, freely and without the safety of her brothers hanging over her head.

She had to want to be with him because she cared about him, not out of some misguided need to sacrifice herself for her brothers. And because of all this, it meant that every second she was outside of his home alone, she was at risk. He had no way of knowing what she would do in an attempt to reach or rescue her brothers. The idea terrified him.

The thought of losing Harper sent a chill down his spine. She no doubt assumed he wanted her only for her body, but she couldn't be more wrong. In the short time he'd had with her, he'd realized that she was a female unlike any other. She wasn't just intelligent— she was *brilliant*, with so much potential. She was also loyal, brave, compassionate, and sensual. Everything a male like him could dream of and hope for in a mate.

"Your latest assignment?" A familiar voice broke through his brooding thoughts. Familiar because it sounded much like his own. He swiveled in his anti-gravity chair.

His twin, Soren, stood there looking amused. He wore a human three-piece gray suit, which meant he must have recently come from his duties as ambassador.

"Soren, what are you doing here?" With a subtle gesture, Sef switched off all the surveillance screens behind him. He didn't want Soren to realize he was spying on his own house.

"I agreed to show Bianca one of the Centers here in the Midwest."

Sef raised a brow in challenge. "She's already visited the Center near Monterey several times since you moved there. Why would you bring her to Kansas City?"

His brother chuckled. "Perhaps I came to tell you that Mother and Father have left Krina recently. They intend to move to Earth and will be planet side in a few days."

"What? I thought they planned to stay there for another decade, along with the first wave of colonists."

Soren laughed. "That worried, eh? Mother promised me she wouldn't try to hook you up with any females we know. She didn't want to wait for the colonist groups. She wanted to come sooner."

Sef stifled a groan. His mother had been trying to arrange a match for both him and his brother for the last thousand years. Soren, by claiming a human charl, had escaped their mother's plans, but that left

Sef all on his own to face her well-intentioned schemes.

"So..." Soren focused on him. "Who were you watching?" He nodded to the blank screens behind Sef.

"No one."

"No one? Come, brother, you know me better than that. I won't judge. Have you become besotted with a human?" Soren pulled up a chair and leaned in. "I will tell no one, not even Mother. Twins' honor." He raised his hand and touched his heart.

"Twins' honor?" Sef hadn't heard that phrase in a long time. It was something from their boyhood, a promise they'd made to each other to reflect the need for ultimate trust.

"You have my word. Now, tell me." Soren kept his voice low because Sef's office wasn't separated by walls from the other guardians of the Center working in nearby cubicles.

"I had an assignment in Kansas, the one I told you about. There were two suspected resistance leaders there. They owned a bar and were hosting meetings in the back storeroom. It turned out to be more serious than we suspected. They were getting ready to work with a human who knows one of our kind, who was going to help them acquire bombs to break down our walls, steal our tech, and expose the Center to the general public."

"What?" Soren paled. "That's serious."

"But they also had a younger sister. She's..." He cleared his throat and continued. "I got too close. I brought her here when I took her brothers into custody. I messed up."

Soren was quiet, but Sef didn't see any flicker of judgment or disapproval in his brother's face.

"Messed up how, exactly?"

"I desire her, *deeply*, as I've never desired any other female. It's like a madness possesses me whenever I'm near her. I told her that if she agreed to submit to me, to be my charl, then I would keep her brothers from having their memories erased."

"Is that something you can promise?" Soren inquired.

"If they can cooperate and prove to be nonviolent, which I believe may be possible with a little time, I can keep them safe. Detained, but safe. Eventually they could be released."

Soren leaned back in the chair, their gazes locked. "Sef, let me give you some advice. Seducing one's charl without securing her trust only goes so far. Females never truly submit, not like you expect. They can be sweet and willing to bow to our dominant tendencies, but a female will always be in charge of her own life, and you shouldn't want it any other way. If you resist letting her have her own life, it will hurt you both. You must be ready to give her the freedom to walk away if she can't be happy with you. I know you hold on to our traditions of taking what you want, but if she can't be happy, you won't be either. And that is one thing you cannot live with. So woo her, seduce her, make sure she is hopelessly in love with you, but most importantly, earn her trust, then give her the key to her cage. She may surprise you by not flying away."

Sef closed his eyes, drew in a deep breath, and opened his eyes again.

"Tell me, does Bianca make you this crazed? Even when I'm furious, I want to take her to bed and fuck her and then hold her close just to reassure myself she is still in my arms."

"Have you drunk from her yet?" Soren asked.

Sef nodded. "Yes, I know I shouldn't have, given that I was still pretending to be human, but she was so tense the first time we mated that she needed help to relax since she was so small and had trouble accommodating me, so I bit her."

"And now you are addicted," Soren guessed. "The same was true of me with Bianca. The bloodlust grows stronger over time, but trust me, so does your control. Your desire to protect her will overrule any desire to drink too much."

Sef nodded. "I have no doubts about my control, but I can't imagine letting her go."

"She must be special."

"You have no idea." He spun toward his desk and

pulled up copies of the blueprints she'd made on the screen. "Look at these." Soren slid his chair closer so they were sitting side by side.

"They're very unique," Soren said. "But they seem very rough. Who designed them? Does Korum have an apprentice?"

"They're Harper's."

A look of shock swept over his twin's features. "But...how? These designs feature components of our science. Even understanding the basic concepts is..."

"Too advanced for a human?" Sef finished smugly.

"Yes. All the humans' top scientists who have been trying to understand our technology haven't come this close. So how?" Soren repeated, still closely studying the designs.

"I have no idea. She's had no access to our technology, only secondhand information and what little has been seen by their media. She came up with these based entirely on observation and supposition. But she suffers from severe dyslexia."

"What is that?"

"A human neurological condition that makes reading very difficult and, in her case, painful. I was thinking of having our biologists look at her and see if they could do something to help her."

Soren nodded. "You should. Imagine what she could accomplish without that limitation. She could be working alongside Korum or other engineers."

"That is what I was thinking. She could point toward the future of humans, one where we work alongside them and no longer against them." It had long been a desire among the Krinar to find such enlightened humans, ones who wanted to improve their world to the benefit of all. Before meeting Harper, Sef had lost all hope of seeing that side of humanity. But perhaps Harper was the beginning of the change.

"Driana, one of our best biologists, can relocate here for a while to check into your female's condition. She'll be teaching in the fall at Princeton, but travel between New Jersey is easy with our spacecrafts. I would be happy to contact her." Soren touched his shoulder, and a deep joy surged between them.

"Thank you," Sef said, hoping his brother could feel his own echo of joy through their bond.

Soren grinned mischievously. "I'm happy you found a human mate. Mother will find out eventually, like she did with me and Bianca. I swear to keep my mouth shut, but once she arrives, I doubt you'll be able to keep the secret for long."

"True." Sef winced, knowing how perceptive their mother was. "I guess I need to woo my rebellious charl sooner rather than later."

"Why don't you take her out to dinner with Bianca and me tonight?" Soren offered. "Bianca can perhaps dispel some of her fears about what it means to be a charl and show your Harper the positives of belonging to a Krinar male."

"That's not a bad idea." Sef nodded. "Very well. Let's go for it. We'll see you this evening."

Soren grinned, clapping Sef's shoulder again as he stood. "This should be fun." He left Sef's office, though Sef wondered just how much fun Soren would have at his expense tonight.

———

HARPER HAD SHOWERED AND FELT REFRESHED. SHE dressed in clean clothes from her belongings, which had arrived in featureless boxes an hour ago. Now she was ready to face the problem of being incarcerated by an alien she'd once had feelings for and was now determined to hate until the day she died.

"Linda?" she called out while in the kitchen again.

"Yes, Harper?"

"I need to make updates to your system. How would I do that?"

"Updates?" Linda's confusion was clear. "I require no updates. I am an ever-adjusting operating platform that that exists from a central control core."

Now we're getting somewhere. Harper chuckled and rubbed her hands together like a cartoon villain. "Linda..." Harper paced the length of the kitchen. "Exactly how is your platform linked to the central core?"

"Via QER signals."

"What are those?"

"Quantum entanglement receptors. The closest approximation would be sound waves or radio waves, but it is far too complex for human understanding," the voice responded.

"Right..." Harper drawled out the word sarcastically. She actually understood what quantum entanglement was, on a theoretical level anyway. "And where is your central core physically located?"

"My central core is installed in Sef's hand. It draws additional resources from a common data storage facility, which links to databases used by all Krinar Centers."

"Okay, so it's part cloud data storage and part physical storage. So your program is installed in his hand? How does that even work?" She wrinkled her nose, now picturing Sef as some sort of cyborg.

"The nanocytes in the Krinar work using nanorobotic technology. The implants in their palms can interact with virtually all forms of Krinar technology."

Holy cow... Harper took a moment to wrap her brain around that and then posed another question. "All right, these nanocytes. How do they work?"

"That information is classified." Linda's prompt reply shut down Harper's hopes. But she at least had one more bit of the puzzle pieced together.

"Linda, I don't have a core or whatever like Sef, so why do you respond to me?"

"You have been designated as his charl. I will provide food, drink, clothing, and any entertainment you wish. I have more than seven hundred channels of entertainment available, and I have determined your preferences with an estimated seventy-eight percent accuracy. Would you like to hear some music?"

Country music suddenly filled the room. A man was crooning about losing his dog and his girlfriend and his truck.

"Well that falls firmly within the remaining twenty-two percent of things I don't prefer," said Harper with a sarcastic chuckle.

"I'm sorry. Given the place of your birth and our current location, I believed that style of music would appeal to you most. I will adjust as I gain more information about you."

"So...you keep on adjusting these preferences over time, huh?" Harper tapped her chin, thinking about how advanced the predictive behavior models were in Krinar tech.

"That is correct."

She suddenly grinned. "Actually, when Sef returns, I'd like you to play some heavy metal music at a high volume. It's his favorite." She bit her lip to keep from laughing.

"That seems unlikely, based on his past preferences. He has never requested me to play such music for him before." Linda sounded mildly perplexed.

Harper plopped down on the sofa, feeling smug. "He acquired a taste for it during his mission, but he's still self-conscious about expressing what he wants, you know? So only play the music when he is alone in the room. It'll put him in a good mood. He also tried some new foods that he fell in love with. I know the recipes. You should surprise him. Sef loves surprises."

"He does?" Linda sounded so gullible.

"Yes, he really does. He's got some new preferences, and you really should update your system with them."

"I will, thank you."

"But let's keep it a secret, okay? I don't want him to know that we are working together. He will be in a better mood if he thinks you came to these conclusions on your own."

"Very well." Linda gave a soft chime, which Harper had figured out was her way of turning off until she was called for again.

Harper leaned forward and unrolled her blueprints across the coffee table. They'd been the first thing she'd looked for after searching for her parents' photos. She hadn't unpacked anything else except for a few clothes and a go-bag she'd hidden under the bed for when it was time to bolt. She had no intention of settling into life here. She would play nice enough until she saw her brothers and figured out a way to bust them out of wherever they were being held.

Yeah, just me against a species that forced the whole planet to surrender. No problem.

By early evening, though, she was growing anxious. What if Sef didn't come back tonight? She usually like being alone, but the thought of imprisonment bothered her, and the feeling continued to grow until it was almost an anxious panic. When Sef finally swept through the front door, she was borderline frantic.

"Where have you been?"

He froze by the front door and stared at her. "I was working."

"I didn't know if you were ever coming back. I was freaking out." She didn't want to admit that part, but it just slipped out.

Sef's sensual lips twitched as though he was fighting off a smile. "Worried about me?"

Harper frowned and crossed her arms over her chest. "Hardly. But if you never came back, I would die trapped in here with just Linda for company."

He glanced around the room and frowned. "You haven't put up any of your art prints."

Was that disappointment she heard in his tone, or was she merely imagining it?

"I was busy."

"Well, that's good, I suppose. I half expected you to tear the house apart looking for a way to escape."

"So you're admitting I'm your prisoner?"

Sef started toward the stairs, and she followed him. "If you wish to think so, you may, but you also agreed to come here and be mine."

"Under *duress*. To save my brothers' *lives*," she snapped. "Don't think I'm just going to surrender to you and go all Stockholm syndrome, buddy."

His lips twitched at her words, but he didn't respond as he headed up the stairs.

He entered his bedchamber and then removed his T-shirt, offering her a view of his fine muscled back. With a careless air, he tossed the shirt to the floor.

What a slob, Harper thought with relish at finding a flaw in this seemingly flawless alien male. Just then, a panel on the base of the nearest wall opened up. A swift little disk-shaped robot, sort of like a Roomba, rolled out, collected the shirt, and returned right back into the wall. Harper leaped onto the bed, gasping in shock.

"What the hell was that?" She stared around the room. She loved machines, but the Roomba thing had just appeared without warning, and it made her worry about what else might come through the walls when she wasn't prepared.

"That was a varduum." He was facing her bare-chested, which made it hard to think.

"That sounds an awful lot like a vacuum. Only our vacuums don't automatically pick up after people." She couldn't help but stare at his broad chest, remembering how warm his skin was as she fell asleep on top of him, her cheek pressed to his heart.

"Where do you think humans came up with the word?" Sef was smirking, and she had to resist the urge to leap off the bed and sock him in the jaw.

"Are you saying the Krinar have been around Earth longer than five years?"

"We have been, but that was a joke." He reached for the fly on his jeans. She turned hastily away, but she didn't want to stop their conversation.

"Ha ha. So how long have you guys been around on Earth?"

"A very long time. Your ancient civilizations viewed us as gods. A few of my kind have observed you over the years to offer insight and sometimes influence humans, but we had strict rules not to reveal our true nature until we announced ourselves five years ago."

Harper plopped down on the edge of the bed. "Wait... You're telling me the Ks have been visiting Earth that long?" Her mind flooded with the myths of the ancient Egyptians, Mayans, Greeks, Romans. There were so many cultures that could have been influenced by the Ks. People like Hercules or Samson might have been a K showing off.

"You don't honestly think the Mayans learned how to build those temples on their own?" He chuckled as though amused by the idea. "And haven't you ever noticed the similarities between the structures in Central America, Egypt, and Myanmar?"

"Wait, didn't the Mayans offer human sacrifices?" She definitely didn't think any society that did that was in any way evolved.

Sef's gaze grew intense. "They did. To my people. The Mayan priests assumed we killed the pretty young men and women who were offered up to us, but all we did was take them as charls and return with them to Krina. These rescued humans allowed us to drink from them."

Harper shivered. "So you do drink blood. You really are space vampires."

His brown eyes darkened with irritation. "We are hardly vampires. Our bodies lack a specific hemoglobin, and blood like yours satisfies those needs. But we no longer require it. We now drink a synthetic blood we developed. Now it's more of a treat we indulge in as needed or as desired." He licked his lips as he said this, and Harper suddenly knew how it felt to be like a canary when a cat stared at it.

"At least you've never bitten me." She reached up to her throat instinctively.

Sef laughed. "That's not exactly true."

Harper's breath hitched. She remembered the hickey on her neck that wasn't a hickey. "You *drank* from me? I didn't consent to that!" She rushed past him to the bathroom to examine her neck. She found no trace of any bite, of course. Enough time had passed for it to heal. It felt like a lifetime ago.

Sef moved behind her in the bathroom and placed one arm around her waist. His other hand reached to touch her neck. Their eyes met in the reflection of the mirror.

"That morning we mated in your office. You were having trouble accepting me inside you because you are so small, and I was afraid I was hurting you. So I bit you here." He rubbed a fingertip over a vein in her neck. "My saliva acted like a drug in your system. Humans feel intense pleasure when our saliva enters their bloodstream. A natural development of our evolution to keep prey docile and relaxed." He continued to brush the side of her neck. "Now it gives us pleasure, and humans as well. But we drink very little, as we do not wish to harm you." Her eyes were still locked on his in the mirror. "I never wanted to harm you. I would not have bitten you if you had not been in pain. But you needed to relax when we had sex."

Harper ran over that day in her mind. She had definitely felt pain at first. She'd been far too nervous to calm down, and what she'd thought had been a love bite had been an *actual* bite.

She turned and faced him; they stood so close that her body brushed against his with each movement. She lifted her wrist to his mouth. "Bite me. I want to feel it now, with a clear head." She had to know if what she'd experienced when she was with him had been all the bite, or if there really had been pleasure just between them. Testing the bite's effect was a good start.

He stepped back. "No."

"Do it. I want to know what it feels like when I don't want to sleep with you."

His lips pursed into a hard line. "That's the problem. You *will* want to sleep with me after the bite. It has an aphrodisiac effect."

She still didn't believe him. Not completely, anyway.

She took another step closer, boxing him in against the bathroom wall. "Sef, I want you to bite me."

He took her wrist, holding it firmly but gently. "And when I do and you suddenly ache for me to be inside you, what then?" His voice was filled with rough desire, and his brown eyes were almost gold. How was that possible?

"I won't," she vowed, but it felt like a lie. Being this close to him, she silently admitted to herself that her body wanted him.

"But if you do?"

"Then you'd better resist, because I don't want you taking me when I'm influenced like that." She was not going to let some alien saliva get the better of her. She would bite her own tongue off before she did that.

Sef slowly raised her wrist to his mouth. "Fine. I'll

do it. This might sting for a second until the saliva hits your system. I will heal your wound afterward to make sure you won't have a scar."

Then before she could change her mind, he bit her.

She yelped, but the pain quickly changed to fascination as Sef sucked at her wrist. It wasn't messy, and he didn't suck her like a vampire in a horror movie either. He sucked like a lover who wanted to leave his mark upon her. Then it hit her, the feeling of something wonderful surging through her body. With every beat of her heart it grew stronger, until the dizzy pleasure and pure intoxication overtook her.

"Oh..." It was all she could say before her knees buckled. Sef released her wrist, licked his lips, and caught her swiftly in his arms. He carried her over to the bed and laid her down with unexpected gentleness. The strange drunken feel of his bite didn't have the wild pleasure she remembered from when they'd made love. It was obvious now, and she couldn't deny it —sex with him was a whole other level of pleasure. It hadn't been all just the bite.

"How do you feel?" he asked.

"Dizzy." She licked her lips. "I never...liked getting drunk. It...scares me..." Words were slow to form, but he patiently waited for her to speak.

"It scares you?"

"I like being in control. Control is safe," she continued. "You don't make mistakes...say or do the wrong thing..."

"You need never worry about that with me, sweetheart. I'll always make sure you're safe."

He brushed her hair back from her face, and the caress felt intensely wonderful.

"Do it again," she said.

"Yes, my little Queenie." He chuckled and stroked her hair over and over. She wanted to shout at him, tell him he had no right to call her that, but the way he touched her felt so good she couldn't find it in her to say the words. Her eyes drifted shut as pleasure rolled through her in foggy waves, carrying her into blissful darkness. His touch was the last thing she felt.

———

SEF WAITED UNTIL SHE WAS ASLEEP, THEN TUCKED HER into bed. She was strong-willed for a human, but she did not have the energy to fight her own exhaustion. His saliva had helped, of course, lulling her to sleep. He was impressed but also disappointed that she had not begged him to take her. But Harper was stubborn if nothing else, and he had to admire that.

"Rest well, my little Queenie." He stood, removed his jeans and boots, and stepped into the bathroom. The moment he entered the shower, a cacophony of loud and horrible sounds filled the bathroom. It was music. Earth music, of the *worst* kind. Like vomit for the ears. Despite dressing like a human biker gang member for the last several missions on Earth, he didn't like this sort of music at all.

"Silence!" he bellowed, his voice echoing off the marble walls.

"Muting," the computer said. "My sensors indicate you are aggravated. Was the music inappropriate?"

"When have I ever suggested that I would enjoy that *racket*?"

"I was informed that your preferences have changed and that you would enjoy this selection of music," the automated voice of his home chimed in.

Informed. By Harper, of course. "Well, I don't. Never play this kind of music again." His ears were still ringing from the terrible sounds.

"Understood." The home system signed off with a faint chime.

So Harper thought she could play around with him? Well turnabout was fair play, as the humans said. He showered, grinning the entire time. Tonight at dinner, he would play her little game and beat her at it.

13

————

Harper stared at the long frost-blue evening gown. The diaphanous silk seemed to flow down her body in waves as it showed off every curve. A long slit on each side of the gown revealed her legs from mid-thigh down to her ankles. She extended one leg, reluctantly admiring the silver sandals that had straps that went halfway up her calves. They were sexy, possibly sexier than a high-heeled shoe would have been, and yet they were a hundred times more comfortable.

Even though she had to admit she looked incredible, she felt naked. She had no bra on underneath the gown, and Sef had given her panties that were as thin as the gown itself. She'd stared at him when he'd given her the underwear, ready to call him a whole host of names for trying to dress her up like a sex doll, but he'd politely insisted that simple cotton panties would not be appropriate under this type of gown, that they'd show up too clearly. After she'd attempted to wear her normal underwear beneath the dress, she'd unfortunately had to agree.

She adjusted her breasts in the bodice, which was a slightly darker shade of blue, and tried not to think about how naked she felt. It was like she was wearing an expensive negligée or something a 1940s starlet would wear to bed.

Sef had changed out of his jeans and T-shirt and into white trousers and a soft sky-blue tunic. It was such a different look than what she was used to. She'd adored him in plaid shirts and jeans, but this...this alien version of him was strangely enticing. Even the soft colors of the white and blue didn't take away from his darkly handsome features.

But it was also a reminder that he wasn't human, that he wasn't the man she'd fallen for back in Lawrence.

"How do I look?" She turned to Sef to gauge his reaction. He was sitting on the edge of his bed, and he twirled a finger, indicating she should spin around. She did, trying not to acknowledge the girlish excitement she felt at the way the skirts fluttered out around her. She'd worn her share of dresses, like any woman, but there was something about this gown that seemed...almost princess-like, yet it was also incredibly sexy in the way it hinted at her body's natural curves and revealed her legs as she walked.

"It will do," Sef said, but she didn't miss the swirling gold in his dark eyes. He liked it. She had a feeling that whenever his eyes turned that honey-gold color, he was turned on.

"If it's not good enough, I could just strip and go naked to dinner," she suggested defiantly. "You Ks don't seem to be bothered by running around practically naked. I've seen photos on the news of how slinky the women dress, those formfitting sheer fabrics..."

Sef stood and came behind her, his hands spanning her waist as he caught hold of her from behind.

"That's because we aren't embarrassed by our bodies. We find no shame in them, no matter what size or shape we are." His gaze met hers in the full-length mirror, and she was shocked at the reminder of how tall and powerful he was. His body dwarfed hers. He could easily overpower her and take her at any time, yet he held her gently, the heat of his body seeping into her skin in the most wonderful way. She *did* feel safe, just as he'd promised her, and it made the hate and anger she felt toward him quake on its foundations.

"But you definitely shouldn't go around naked. You're too tempting for the males of my kind as it is. Another one might snatch you up and carry you off. Then I'd have to fight him for ownership of you."

Ownership of her? That simple comment threw an

entire gas tank on the embers of her fury. "Own me? You don't *own* me!" She spun around and hauled back to punch him. He caught her wrist with one hand, holding her immobile.

"Yes, ownership, Queenie. Until humans can be trusted, you cannot be given equal status. Does that mean I think you are inferior? No. Never. You are as brilliant as you are beautiful, as much as any Krinar woman, but for all practical purposes you are still *mine*." He growled the word in a way that sent shivers down her spine, but they weren't shivers of dread.

Sef lowered his gaze, and she couldn't stop staring at his lips. He moved her back until he had her pinned against the mirror. Despite being trapped, her body throbbed with hunger as well. If he took her now, she wouldn't fight him. She wanted it. She wanted him to claim her. She ached for the pleasure his body could give her, but she also yearned for that intimacy that came after, the whispers in the dark, the gentle lacing of fingers, and the nuzzling of faces as they lay in one another's arms.

His lips barely touched hers, a ghost of a kiss that seemed to go on forever.

Please...don't stop. The words echoed inside her head, but she didn't dare speak them aloud. She wasn't going to beg him. She wasn't.

His hand cupped the back of her neck and fisted in the strands of her hair. He licked at the seam of her lips, and she opened for him. He thrust his tongue inside, showing her exactly what would happen between them if she only asked him. She tried desperately to curl a leg around his lean hips so she could rub herself against his hard body and the bulge that was digging into her stomach. He let her, but he didn't move to cup her bottom or to hike her skirts up, which made her want to scream in frustration.

Just take me already.

Instead, he continued to kiss her in the most devastating way until she was wet and desperate. Then he released her and stepped back, his calm seemingly restored.

"I think it's time to go," he said, his voice slightly breathless.

"Just a minute. I need to fix my hair." *And fix my sanity,* she thought darkly. This K was a menace to her self-control. She turned her attention back to the mirror, trying to run a brush through her hair, which was now a tumble of wild waves.

"Leave it. I like your hair down. You look like I've just taken you to bed for hours," Sef said with a lazy, satisfied grin.

She scowled. "Yes, well, if you're having me dress up nice, I'm not going to leave my hair a mess just so you can act smug around me." She used four bobby pins to make a quick but elegant chignon from a ponytail. She was relieved that he had brought all of her things from home, everything from art prints all the way down to bobby pins. When she was done, she turned back to him.

"Where are we going tonight?" she asked as they left the house.

"To a local restaurant in the middle of the Center."

This was the first time she'd had a proper glimpse of the inside of a K Center, and she couldn't help but be impressed. There were houses everywhere, but they were built far apart, with many trees and flowers around to make it feel woodsy and natural, rather than urban. She liked that. No skyscrapers or buildings above two stories were nearby.

"We prefer to build out rather than up. We enjoy our personal space," Sef explained as he took her arm. They walked down a lovely garden path toward a distant cluster of colorful buildings. She had to admit, what she'd seen so far of the Center was beautiful. It didn't look secretive or dangerous. There were no weapons, no soldiers—it just looked like a peaceful little corner of a neighborhood. The only thing different was the plants.

"What kind of trees are those?" She pointed to a group of trees with rainbow-colored trunks.

"Those are palazzo trees." Sef led her off the path toward the nearest tree and smiled. "You can touch it—it's perfectly safe."

Unable to resist, she reached out and placed a palm

on the bark. It was smooth, like birch. The colors on the bark were striped in reds, greens, blues, and purples.

"How does it have so many colors?"

"There are different levels of acidity within the bark that react to oxygen. As they grow and mature, the acidity fluctuates and the bark changes color. On my home planet, they tend to be black with white stripes, but here...the different composition of the soil, water, and light creates a rainbow of colors. They are beautiful, aren't they?"

She agreed and stroked the tree a moment longer. Sef led her back to the garden path. It was odd to think that something from his planet could change that much here, and in her opinion, for the better.

"We have many beautiful trees and plants. Most are perfectly safe. We brought them with us." He waved an arm around them. "But we have Earth trees and plants too. Just over there are maple, elm, sycamore, and your mighty oak." He nodded toward the surrounding woods, and she saw he was right. Normal trees, the ones she recognized, were interspersed between the palazzo trees.

Something occurred to her. "I doubt those were there when you set up the Center, and I doubt you brought full-grown trees on spaceships. Why do I get the feeling that if I cut down that oak, I'd count only five rings?"

Sef smiled. "Very observant. Yes. We were able to accelerate their growth significantly. It took only two years to reach their current size, at which point the process was stopped."

"They look so ordinary compared to the trees from Krina. Like humans compared to Ks, I suppose," she said, her heart dropping inside her chest. Humans were so unexceptional compared to the Krinar.

Sef pulled her to a stop, and she faced him in confusion. "You think you are ordinary?"

"Well, yeah. I mean, I'm not blind. I've seen Krinar women. Humans must seem boring and unimpressive by comparison."

Sef's brown eyes were soft and dark as cinnamon. He cupped her face in one hand, and she didn't pull away. The spell of his gaze locked her into place.

"Humans are anything but ordinary. Do you know how amazing it is that your species has progressed as quickly as you have?" He smiled then, the expression tender, so tender that it made the knot of black anger inside her start to crumble at the edges. "Most of the worlds we've seeded seem to have plateaued in a preindustrial state. Some are peaceful, others aren't, but they all seem to be lacking something that your people have in great abundance—imagination. You have but the blink of an eye and your lives are over, yet you dare to dream bigger and brighter each day. You live fearlessly, and you create and inspire others to be better.

You build upon the dreams of the ones who came before you. My people live long lives, and while we have accomplished much, your potential outshines even us. We...all of my people, we have such high hopes for you. Once you see the universe as we do, then you'll be ready for our technology. And then you will truly be free."

"That could take a long time—to see the world as you do, I mean." She lowered her gaze, feeling oddly shy as she spoke so openly of something so deep. Seth might never have existed, but this was the man she had fallen for, this man who saw beyond what most men did. A man who saw *her*.

"And then I wonder, if more humans opened their hearts, believed in us as well as themselves, what wonders could our races achieve together? That is why I am asking you to open yourself to me, Harper. And to my people."

She lifted her gaze to his as he said her name. His plea was so gentle and so earnest. But that black knot inside her, the one that held her back because she could see the other side of the K equation, flared with fresh pain.

"But my brothers..."

"They have a choice. Let me show you my world. Then you can convince them to open their hearts and minds. They can be given freedom again, but they have to trust my people. When I captured them, it was because they were working with a dangerous man, one who was planning to plant bombs on the walls of this very Center. It could have killed my people and any humans nearby. Your brothers were reluctant to engage with this human, but they eventually agreed to work with him, accepting the potential loss of life. That was why I had to intervene. If Mason and Liam cannot learn to trust me and my people, then we must protect my people and yours. I understand their need to resist, to fight, but it is misguided and futile. We aren't here to hurt humans. We want to help. The sooner you can believe in us, the sooner we can let you become partners with us and not adversaries."

What he was saying made sense, but how could she know he really meant it?

"I'll try," she finally said.

"Good." Sef leaned down and pressed his lips to hers in a sweet kiss. He gripped her hips, holding her tightly to him as the kiss turned hot and intense in seconds. She moaned against him, wanting more and inwardly cursing when he stopped and pulled back.

"As much as I would love to continue this," he said, mere inches from her lips, "we shouldn't be late. They're waiting for us."

"Who?" She clung to his arm as they started walking again.

"My brother and his mate. I thought you might like to meet a human charl and ask her any questions you have. You may have some time alone with her if you don't trust her to answer honestly in front of us."

"Wait, your brother? You mean Ambassador Soren?"

She couldn't fully wrap her mind around that. He was one of the most famous Ks on the planet, aside from Korum, who had married his charl, Mia, not too long ago in a televised ceremony. That had been a huge deal. But Soren...wow, he was a political rock star.

"Soren has a charl?" She kept her voice down as they reached a cluster of buildings. One was definitely a restaurant of sorts.

Several Krinar were dining outside, looking relaxed, pleasant, and happy. They were so different from the aliens who had burst into her brothers' bar. Those Krinar with white uniforms and weapons had been terrifying. Here she was glimpsing everyday Krinar life, and it looked very much like what humans would be doing on a day like this. The women wore lovely clothes, either fashionable pants and tops or dresses, and Harper felt like she had definitely over-dressed. It was like showing up in an evening gown to a summer barbecue.

She leaned into him and whispered, "Sef, I don't think my dress is all that appropriate." The heat of his body sank into hers, warming her as her skin chilled in the evening air.

"You are dressed exactly the way I wish you to be. I want to show you off in front of my people."

"Yeah, but"

He spun and caught her in his arms, silencing further protests with a kiss. She gasped as he claimed her mouth, and none too chastely. When he released her, she clamped her thighs together to hide her arousal. She would soak the thin panties he'd given her to wear if he didn't stop this.

"Come, I see my brother over there." Sef escorted her past the Krinar dining outside as he led her into the restaurant.

Harper's face flushed, but she couldn't stop reacting to him. How was she going to implement her plan if he kept making her own body betray her?

14

———

"Soren," Sef called out. His warm tone relaxed Harper a little, but her stomach still fluttered wildly as she saw the famous Krinar waiting for them at a table. The Krinar male stood and embraced his twin. Without Sef's disguise, it was hard to tell the two apart.

"Soren, this is Harper King." Sef gently pulled her in front of him, a proud smile on his face that confused her. Why was he proud?

"Ms. King, you have no idea the pleasure I have of meeting the female who has claimed my brother's heart."

"Soren." Sef's tone hardened. But Harper was still caught on Soren's words. Did that mean Sef truly cared about her? Or that Soren assumed that she was in love with Sef?

"It's nice to meet you." She held out a hand, but Soren politely shook his head.

"I'm afraid if I touched you, that would upset my brother. We males are far too possessive." Soren chuckled.

"Oh...right." She dropped her hand, and Sef leaned into her and pressed his lips to her temple while eyeing his brother. It felt good, *too* good. She knew she should pull away, but she didn't.

"I would like you to meet my charl and wife, Bianca Wells."

Harper paled. "*The* Bianca Wells? President Wells's daughter? You married her?" Harper couldn't believe that wasn't international news, but then again, maybe Soren and Bianca had kept it quiet for a reason.

"Yes," Soren chuckled. "She's my wife in the human fashion, but also my charl." He looked over her shoulder at Sef. "She wanted to wait, but you know how impatient I can be."

Sef shook his head, a mirthful twinkle in his eyes. "I do indeed." The three of them walked over to Soren's table.

A beautiful blonde woman with stunning hazel-green eyes rose to her feet and immediately hugged Harper. "Hello. I'm Bianca."

"I'm Harper. It's an honor to meet you."

"Please, the honor is mine. Sef is quite intense, so I had to see the woman who tamed him." Bianca winked at her. Harper couldn't believe she was meeting two of the most famous people on the planet.

"What's it like being the daughter of a president?" Harper asked, then blushed. "Sorry, I guess you get asked that a lot."

Bianca shrugged. "Family wise it's no different than before. He's my dad. But I put a lot of focus on making my life mean something more to the world than just being a president's daughter."

"Oh, I didn't mean" Harper stammered.

Bianca chuckled. "Don't worry about it. What I mean is that I don't want you to see me as anything special." She gestured for them to sit. "I work just like everyone else, and I strive to make the world a better place in my own way."

"That's wonderful," Harper said. "I admire that. A lot of people in your position might not care."

Bianca shrugged. "I lost my mom when I was young. That put things in perspective, you know? About what's really important in life."

"I understand that more than you know. My parents died on K-Day."

"Oh my God. How?"

"A bridge collapsed during the Panic. It changed how I saw the world."

Bianca reached out and touched her arm, giving it a gentle squeeze. "I'm so sorry."

Bianca and Harper sat across from one another, and their Krinar lovers took opposite seats.

"So how did you meet Sef?" Bianca asked as she looked over one of the menus.

"I..." She looked at Sef, and he gave a slight nod. Did that mean she could be honest?

"We met at the bar Harper's older brothers own. I was investigating anti-K rebel activity," Sef explained when she continued to hesitate. "I arrested her brothers."

The menu fell from Bianca's hands. "You did *what*?"

Sef coughed as his face darkened into a ruddy color. "Well...it's the truth. It's how we met."

Harper thought about saying more, divulging Sef's betrayal, but it wouldn't change anything, and she didn't think it was worth ruining their dinner over. She was curious to explore Krinar cuisine, and more importantly, she wanted to ask Bianca more about being a charl. Starting an argument might deprive her of that opportunity.

"You're not off to the most auspicious start, brother," Soren chuckled. He grunted and glanced down at something under the table. Harper suspected that Sef had kicked him under the table. They reminded her far too much of Mason and Liam. Even as grown men in their thirties, they still tussled like puppies, kicking and shoving and tackling each other when the opportunity arose. Males were the same in every species, it seemed.

A waiter approached their table, holding up his right palm as he recited the specials. It looked like he had written something on his hand. She caught the faint blue glow just above his hand, and she realized he must have a central core computer implant in his hand like Sef. Harper looked helplessly to Sef, not knowing what any of the food was. He leaned in close, his alluring scent wrapping around her.

"I would suggest trying the aquine salad with toast. It has crumbled cheese similar to feta, and it's sprinkled with dried fruits that are like your Earth cranberries."

"No surf and turf option?" she quipped.

Bianca, who had been drinking her water, choked and started laughing.

"Oh my God, I'm so glad I'm not the only one who misses *real* meat." She nudged Soren with her elbow. "When we get back to California, I want a cheeseburger. I don't care what you have to do to get me one."

Soren flashed Bianca a smile. "Anything you wish." Harper could tell he meant it.

Harper followed Sef's advice and ordered the aquine salad. She watched the waiter closely, seeing the glow of hologram text in the Krinar language hovering just above his skin as he recorded their orders. What would it take to get Sef to show her his hand? She wanted to know exactly how the central core technology worked. Maybe after dinner she could use her feminine wiles to convince him.

"So, Harper, Soren says you're from Kansas?"

"Yes, from a town called Lawrence." Harper tried some of the wine Sef poured for her. It was sweet, almost like a rosé but slightly more fruity, and the alcoholic content seemed lower. She'd noticed that the Krinar didn't seem to bother with heavy drinking.

"What do you do? Job wise, I mean?" Bianca asked.

"I'm...I mean, I *was* a mechanic."

"You are an engineer," Sef corrected, reaching out to curl his fingers around hers. She was tempted to pull away, but dammit, she liked how warm his hand was. His words were absolute and certain, but his touch wasn't about control—it was about comfort.

"I guess I am, I just don't have a college degree. Self-taught," she amended. "I owned an auto shop. My brothers owned the bar."

"Wow, an engineer. That's impressive." Bianca's praise made Harper's head spin a little.

"What about you?" Harper asked her.

"I'm a marine biologist. I just got my degree a few months ago. I'm working in an aquarium in Monterey Bay."

"No kidding. Do you work with the sea otters there?" Harper had always loved otters. Living in

Kansas, she'd seen some river otters, but those were quite different from sea otters.

"Don't get her started on otters," Soren teased. "She'll never stop."

Bianca punched his shoulder and laughed. Their affectionate teasing made Harper's chest ache. That was what she'd always imagined she'd have with the man she loved. But could Sef ever give her that? She feared she had lost all chance of ever having that kind of relationship by making her devil's bargain.

By the time the food arrived, she was feeling rather pitiful, and she didn't like indulging in bouts of self-pity. Her parents hadn't raised her to be like that. Sef released her hand as the waiter placed their food on the table. But he didn't ignore her; rather, his hand moved under the table to touch her thigh. It startled her so much she nearly jumped. His large hand curved around her thigh, stilling her, his fingertips stroking the sensitive parts of her skin. Her body hummed with arousal, the kind she could just keep control of as long as he didn't—

His hand slipped higher up, almost touching the juncture of her thighs. Dear God, was he going to get her hot and bothered right there in front of his brother and his brother's wife? In a public restaurant?

She blamed the slit in the dress. It made it way too easy for him to reach her bare skin. Which he no doubt knew, since he'd picked out the damn thing. His fingers drew slow circular patterns on her inner thigh, and though it was difficult, she did her best to ignore him while she ate. The salad was really good. It still didn't compare to a good old greasy cheeseburger, in her opinion, but it was certainly an interesting choice. As Soren explained to her, aquine was a type of edible flower. The petals were plucked while in bloom and sprinkled over the salad. When she tasted the bright-purple petals, they were a lot like lemon. The citrus flavor blended well with the freshly cut romaine lettuce and the light balsamic dressing.

Soren and Sef talked while she and Bianca ate their dinner, mostly in silence. The brothers discussed their friends back on Krina and laughed about old memories that were from thousands of years ago. Harper hadn't thought to ask how old Sef was, but she made a note to inquire later. When dessert came to the table, Harper had grown used to Sef's teasing touches and could almost ignore how inappropriate it was. She focused on the small parfait-shaped glass that was filled with a creamy substance that reminded her of sorbet with tiny pieces of fruit in it. It was *delicious*.

"I think this is my favorite Krinar food," Harper said, and Sef chuckled.

"I shall remember that. It's called hoola ice. You can ask Linda for it at any time."

"Hoola ice?" Harper repeated, determined to remember the name.

"Wait, who's Linda?" Bianca asked.

"My central core device at home," Sef explained.

"You named yours?" Bianca looked to Soren. "Can we do that too?"

Soren looked puzzled. "It never occurred to me that you would want to. Is it normal for humans to name their machines?"

"It is if they talk to us." Bianca winked at Harper. "Ours has a masculine voice, so I'm thinking Bob...or maybe Eustace or maybe Chris Hemsworth"

Soren cleared his throat. "Bob would be just fine."

Bianca grinned back mischievously at Soren. "Or maybe HAL, like in *2001: A Space Odyssey*, in case Soren gives me a hard time and I want to lock him out of the house."

As the dinner continued, Harper found she really enjoyed Bianca's company and already considered her a friend. She hoped she would get a chance to see more of the other woman. They teased Soren and Sef with their Earth trivia and mentioning their favorite movie stars, using their shared experiences as a code of sorts between them. After all, she understood what Bianca had meant about naming the central core computer HAL, but Soren hadn't. But some references elicited puzzled questions from the Krinar brothers.

"Wait...let me see if I understand this," Soren said as he cut in on Harper and Bianca's discussion of Pop

Rocks. "You put this...crumbling candy into your mouth and it...explodes?"

Harper laughed at Soren's shocked expression. "Not explodes. Pops."

"You find this activity enjoyable?" Sef asked.

"Yeah, it's weird and fun," Harper explained. "The one thing I've always been afraid to try is Mentos and Diet Coke in my mouth. When I was little, my brothers told me it would make my stomach explode, and as stupid as it sounds, I still kind of believe it might be true."

"Me too! Never tried it except in a Diet Coke bottle." Bianca giggled.

"Okay, I'm lost. What are Mentos, and how does a beverage factor in?" Sef asked.

"You put these small Mentos candies into a Diet Coke bottle, and like the second you drop them into the bottle, it shoots up a plume of foam, sometimes as high as ten feet."

"It's really fun. It's a rite of passage for grade school kids," Bianca added.

"Sounds like we missed out on quite the childhood." Sef chuckled as he looked to Soren. They shared a warm, familial smile, and Harper couldn't help but remember what Sef had said about the way their relationship had felt strained after Soren's escape from Zaruth, but it seemed they were growing close again.

"It's time we should retire, Bianca. My parents are arriving tomorrow, and I'm certain Mother will wear you out." Soren stood and pulled Bianca's chair back.

"I'm really not ready to meet the in-laws," Bianca muttered, but she was still smiling. "Harper, it was so nice to meet you. Perhaps you and I could meet tomorrow and explore the Center?"

"She doesn't have her freedom yet," Sef said flatly, dropping his hand from Harper's thigh as he stood.

"Freedom? Wait...what are you talking about?" Bianca looked between Sef and Harper, worry knitting her brows.

"Come, Bianca, I will explain at home," Soren said as tucked her arm in his and gently led her away. Harper listened to the other woman's protests until they exited the restaurant.

"Would it really have been so bad to let me wander around a bit? Bianca's nice, and having a friend here would make me a lot less lonely. And where exactly am I going to go? It's not like I can just waltz out of the Center."

Sef cupped her chin with one hand. "You've done well tonight. I will take you to see your brothers tomorrow morning. After that, we can discuss an outing on your own with Bianca."

Harper bit her tongue. She still couldn't believe how medieval he was behaving when it came to her freedom. Did he honestly think she was dangerous? She wasn't going to hurt any of the Ks.

Of course...if she was able to crack the key to Krinar technology, she could bust out of the Center and rescue her brothers.

"We should go." He offered her his arm, and she took it. They left the restaurant and began walking back through the Center using a different route. Sef showed her all of the strange life of the K Center, from the farmlands to their shopping venues. Though it all looked alien to her, it also looked familiar, and Sef pointed out that human influences were integrated into their designs to make the transition into human society easier. He even brought her to one of their parks, where she saw a few K children playing.

"So few?" She nodded at the handful of children playing on the jungle gym equipment that look like a very fancy version of what human kids played on.

"We don't conceive easily, and given our lifespan, it's wise not to overpopulate. Most of my people only ever have a few children over the millennia. It makes them very precious." Sef's lips curved in a tentative smile as he watched a little girl chase a bigger boy around.

"Do you have any children?" Harper asked, her heart tight as she wondered if perhaps he'd had a wife and possibly children in the past.

"No. I've never taken a mate or a charl, and I've never had children."

"Do you *want* children?" she asked.

"I do. Very much. It's strange. I've lived eight thousand years, and until now I've had no desire for children, but all that's changed." Sef looked her way, his gaze unbearably tender. "I want children with you."

"W-with m-me?" she stammered. He pulled her into his arms, kissing her gently, sweetly.

"Yes, if you want them, it would be a great honor to have them with you." She saw the open sincerity in his eyes as he said this. "Our people are still trying to find a way to make our mating with humans compatible. It is a genetic puzzle, if you will, but we are very close. We predict it will be possible perhaps within the year."

"Wow...kids with the Ks." Harper wasn't sure how she felt about that. Not horrified, but worried. What lives would those children have as half-human? Would their lifespans be different? Would they be viewed as inferior for their human blood? Would full K children not want to play with them? She knew how humans would react, with fear and prejudice, but perhaps the Ks were more accepting. She could only hope they were.

Sef curled an arm around her waist. "I think it's time to go home."

He led them back until they were in familiar territory, and then she recognized the street his house was on. When they got back to Sef's house, he suddenly froze. "Stay behind me."

His tone scared her. "What? Why?"

"Someone is in my house. Linda did not alert me of an intrusion."

"Who is it?" she asked as he crept toward the door, still shielding her. He curled his hand around the knob and pulled hard and fast, whooshing the door open. There was a long moment of silence, but she couldn't see around his tall muscled body to tell who or what was inside.

"*Mother?*" Sef said in shock.

15

His mother was seated on his couch, and his father was in the kitchen preparing two glasses of Krinar wine.

"Sef, my dear," Sarina said in Krinar. Her eyes widened as she noticed who was behind him.

"Who is this?" His mother stood, her pale rose gown displaying her natural beauty. She looked as young as Sef and Soren, even though she had to be older than them.

"This," he said as he gently pried Harper off his back and guided her in front of him, "is Harper. My charl."

"You have a charl?" His mother's head tilted slightly, puzzled but not displeased.

"It's a recent development." He felt his face flush with embarrassment. No matter how old he was, explaining his romantic entanglements to his mother would always be awkward.

"Well, let me see her." Sarina beckoned Harper forward with a nod. Sef felt her stiffen in panic, so he leaned down to whisper in her ear.

"Don't worry. She won't bite."

Harper stepped bravely forward, and Sef closed the door as they all began to gather in the living room.

"Harper?" Sarina asked.

"Yes. Harper King, ma'am." Harper smiled, but Sef saw the worry on her face.

"Ma'am? Oh, my dear child, call me Sarina." His mother smiled broadly, and her brown eyes twinkled with curiosity. "Sarket, come and meet your son's charl."

Sarket left the kitchen and offered his wife and Harper a glass of wine.

"It is lovely to meet you, Ms. King," his father replied. His voice was solemn, but Sef knew his father approved, even if he acted distantly polite. "Sef, I hope you don't mind that we invited ourselves in."

"I was wondering how you got in. I have security protocols in place."

His father's lips twitched. "You have lived too long as a guardian. I only needed to tell your system that I was a family member. The system immediately confirmed that and allowed us in."

"Good point. I assumed only enemies would ever

try to breach my home, not family." That was a loop-hole he would have to see to.

His mother's smile faded. "Enemies? Are you expecting trouble here? I thought the Centers were very safe."

"They are, but I am in a dangerous line of work. It is my duty to anticipate threats at all times."

Sarina relaxed a little. "Ah, I see." She turned her attention back to Harper. "Come and sit, Harper. I would like to get to know you better. You must be quite extraordinary to attract my son's interest. He has been alone a *very* long time."

Sef started to go with Harper as she and his mother sat down on the couch, but his father caught his arm. "Let your mother have a few minutes with her. If you sit there brooding about our unexpected arrival, your charl will be nervous."

"I'm not brooding, Father," he protested, then cursed because he sounded like a child.

"Of course not, son," Sarket said with a smirk. He placed a hand on his shoulder. "Now, come and tell me what troubles you. I see quite clearly something is bothering you." They moved into the kitchen, giving his mother and Harper some space.

As always, his father could see right through him.

"My assignment to uncover an anti-K resistance cell met with some unexpected revelations," he explained. "One of them, a clearly dangerous man, said he was working with a K inside our own Center. A K who wants to betray us. That's what has me worried."

"One of our own?" Sarket's eyes widened. "Do you have any idea who?"

"Not yet. I am going to interview the human prisoner I suspect knows the identity of the Krinar betraying us. But the important thing is that we stopped the attack they were planning. Still, this Krinar traitor is a loose end that has to be stopped."

"You strive so hard to protect those around you, all because you failed to protect Soren when he was captured." Sarket's eyes filled with emotion. "But what happened to Soren was not and will never be your fault. You must put it past you."

Sef studied his father, seeing the wisdom in his face.

"I suppose you're right," he admitted. He had served his people for so very long, to the point where he often didn't think about what he wanted for himself...until recently.

Sarket looked to Harper now with approval. "So, you have taken a charl, and just a few months after Soren. I suppose that was a twin decision?"

"Definitely not." Sef briefly turned aside and asked Linda to make two more drinks for him and his father. "But it is an amusing coincidence that we both found females within so short a time."

"How did you meet Harper?"

"Through my assignment. She is the sister of two of the humans I arrested."

Sarket paled. "What? Is she safe? Should I warn your mother?"

"Mother's fine. Harper is not a rebel. In fact, she's more special than you realize." He motioned for his father to come into his office upstairs. He brought up copies of Harper's designs, converted into hologram form.

"What is this?" His father peered closely at the designs, his face illuminated by the blue glow. "You're not saying she designed these?"

"I am. Her understanding of our flying technology is remarkably close, yet she's never been near our technology. She created these based on observation and instinct."

"This is impressive." Sarket's gaze drifted to the designs again before settling on him. "I suspect you are drawn to her because she's like you in many ways."

"Yes and no," Sef confessed. "We share many of the same interests, but she's also very different. She lives life boldly, beautifully. She's shown me how restrained I've lived in all my years. There's a fire in her that burns bright, and despite her small size, she's strong and bold, yet she isn't foolish."

Sarket sipped his drink and smiled warmly. "You

finally found a mate, my son. And she sounds like a perfect match to you in all ways that matter."

Sef agreed. But he didn't tell his father that Harper was here under duress, that she'd only come here to save her brothers from their fate. Sef knew his actions toward her weren't noble, but after what they'd shared, he could not let her go.

"So, you and Mother have officially left Krina? You're not going back?"

"No, we will not return. The future of our people is here now, and we wish to help make it happen. And seeing as how our sons have both settled down with mates with ties to this planet, we see no reason to return to Krina."

"Which Center will you move to? Do you have a specific city in mind, or will you stay here?"

"As to that, I'm not certain." Sarket leaned back against the counter and watched Sarina, who was in an animated conversation with Harper. Harper suddenly burst out laughing, and Sef found himself smiling at her open amusement.

"If you remained in Kansas City, I would not mind," he offered to his father.

Sarket's eyes gleamed with amusement. "Then perhaps we will stay here. I promise to keep your mother away from you and your charl, at least enough so you might have sufficient time alone."

Sef touched his father's shoulder in love and appreciation. It'd been a long time since he'd seen his parents. So many years had been filled with pain and tension after Soren had gone missing. Sef had walked away from his love of engineering to pursue what he believed to be his duty, but now that he was with Harper, he saw a future where he could let go of all that and return to something he adored almost as much as his rebellious charl.

"Well, I think your mother has told quite enough stories about you to Harper. Why don't we go rescue her?" Sarket suggested.

"Agreed." They walked over to the sitting room, and Sarket caught his wife's attention.

"Oh, it seems I'm being summoned," Sarina teased and opened her arms. "May I hug you, Harper? That is what humans do in greeting, isn't it?"

Harper laughed. "It's fine." She got up and embraced Sarina. Harper was so short compared to his mother, who stood at just over six feet, but it didn't seem to bother Harper at all.

An odd, fuzzy feeling swelled inside his chest. It wasn't an unwelcome feeling at all, but the more he watched his parents with Harper, the stronger it became, like coming home to everything he loved, everything that felt right.

After they bid his parents good night, he locked the front door and turned to Harper. She was putting the used glasses on the kitchen counter, looking puzzled.

He would have to explain to her that they didn't have a traditional dishwasher. There were cleansing units inside the wall for both clothing and dishes, neither of which needed water.

Sef walked over to her, and before she could react, he scooped her up in his arms and carried her up the stairs.

"Sef, what—?" she started, but he silenced her with a kiss. Soon he had her in his room and laid her down upon the bed, rolling on top of her.

Her lips softened beneath his and parted so he could taste the sweetness of the wine upon her tongue. He fisted his hand in her hair, gently coiling his fingers over and over through the silken strawberry-blonde strands. They covered the bed like pools of afternoon sunlight, which only made his hunger to kiss her stronger. Harper curled an arm around his neck, her fingers playing with his hair at the base of his neck. It sent a wave of tingles down his spine.

He groaned in delight, more than ready to worship her for her natural sensual thoughtfulness. He moved his lips down her throat, then nibbled her collarbone playfully before he ripped the slender straps of her gown so that the filmy frost-blue fabric exposed her perfect breasts. She threw her head back, clawing at him as he sucked a pale-pink nipple between his lips.

A soft, sensual purr of pleasure escaped from her as he suckled at the other nipple, until both peaks were hard and her breasts were heavy in his palms as he kneaded them gently.

"Oh God... Oh God...," Harper panted as he shifted down her body and grabbed the fabric of her dress, shredding the dress open right up to her waist.

He pushed her thighs apart and bent his head to her core. She still wore the whisper-thin panties he'd given her, and he grinned wickedly as he pulled them to the side to explore her folds. She was already wet, the dark-pink center of her gleaming with arousal. He flicked his tongue along the inside of her thigh, and she yelped.

He then moved his tongue directly against her core and pushed it inside. She nearly leaped off the bed, as though an electric shock had pulsed through her. He chuckled and used his arms to pin her thighs open to keep her secure on the bed so he could play with her. He pulled her panties tight, knowing it would put more pressure on her clit while he continued to thrust his tongue in and out of her.

"Sef...I can't," she whispered. "Please, let me come."

"Not yet, Queenie," he growled. "You're not ready."

Sweat dewed on her skin as she struggled to contain the swell of ecstasy he knew had to be building inside her.

"Please... I am... Let me...," she begged.

"Remember this, Harper. Remember how good it

feels to have me fucking you. And I haven't even bitten you. I can go all night."

He pushed two fingers into her slit now, stretching her. He pumped his fingers inside her, then ripped her panties off and opened his trousers. He should have stripped off the rest of his clothes, but he couldn't wait. The primal part of him had taken over. He thrust into her, and her back arched, the torn gown rippling like moonlit water around them on the bed. He gripped her hips and sat back on his heels, watching the beautiful display of his charl as she started to climb higher toward a climax.

Harper fisted the sheets, then grabbed his wrists, digging her fingers into his skin as she thrashed beneath him. For such a tiny creature, she was impressively strong. He pounded into her, unleashing his pent-up desires as he claimed her, mated with her fiercely. He never wanted her to forget this moment, how explosive it was when they came together over and over.

"Come, Queenie. Come now." He pumped into her, riding her harder as she screamed in pleasure.

His body tightened, and an explosive climax shot through him. He roared out his pleasure, delighting in the soft, pliant body of his mate beneath him. Then he collapsed on top of her, catching himself just in time to keep from crushing her. He leaned his forearms on either side of her head and pressed kisses down upon the crown of her hair. Harper let out a shivery sigh, her thighs falling loosely open as her strength failed her.

He knew she was exhausted, but the night was far from over. He caught his breath and then pulled out of her and sat up. Then he stripped the rest of his clothes off and removed what remained of her dress until she lay gloriously naked beside him. They faced each other, both breathing raggedly. He slid her closer to him, cupping the soft curves of her ass, and he lifted her leg over into his thigh, curling an arm around her waist. Then he used his hand to guide his cock back inside her.

"How are you hard again?" she gasped as she opened her legs wider. The feel of her around him, tight and hot, was true ecstasy to him. She made him feel safe somehow, even though he was the one who was supposed to be protecting her. He cupped the back of her neck and massaged her tight muscles beneath his fingers.

"Being able to claim you over and over is one of the benefits of being of my species." He pulled almost all the way out of her and rammed back in a little harder. Her inner walls fluttered around him as though trying to draw him in.

"That's a...definite perk," Harper admitted, her words breathless as she placed her palms on his chest.

His skin burned at the contact, and he moved more urgently inside her than he had before, their gazes locked. A quiet passion, something deeper than lust and desire, shimmered between them like a misty rain after a long drought. He was hungry for it, for *her*, craving that intense connection that used to scare him in the past. He never wanted this before, but now he craved it wildly, madly. There could be no other female for him now. Harper was his world.

Pleasure pulsed inside him like the solar flares off an unstable star. Harper's face lifted up to his as she moved with him, their bodies rocking together in a rhythm older than recorded history, perhaps time itself. For so long he had indulged only in lust and savage desires with hard and frantic couplings. But now, a sweet desperation came with his thrusts, and her excited pants and soft, dreamy gaze suspended them in a space somewhere between breaths, outside of reality.

They climaxed together, a perfect union of what burned between them. An endless spark, a rippling wave, and a delicious shiver moved from her into him, as though her warm afterglow had spread into him.

"What we have," he murmured, still stroking the back of her neck, "this is rare. So very rare." *So rare it's worth fighting for,* he added silently. Maybe someday she would understand the choices he'd made, why he'd used her brothers to make her come with him. Maybe someday she wouldn't hate him. Maybe someday she just might love him the way that he loved her.

The thought came so naturally that he didn't immediately realize what had happened. When he did fully understand the change in his heart, his heart trembled. He *loved* his little human. Somehow, in just a week, he'd fallen under Harper's spell.

"Harper, I..." But the words wouldn't come. Not because he was afraid to say them, but because he knew she wasn't ready to hear them, and he didn't feel he had the right to say them, not until he'd earned her trust.

She snuggled deeper into him, sharing body heat. "Yes?"

He marveled at the power she held over him. He would do anything for her...except let her go. "We will see your brothers first thing in the morning, as I promised."

"Thank you," she whispered against his neck.

He savored her presence, pressing a kiss to her forehead. "I want you to be happy, and I want you to believe me when I say my people and yours can be allies, even friends. The life I envisioned for us, not just as a couple but as a human and a Krinar together, is one of joy and equality and freedom. But I need you to trust me, Harper. Can you do that?"

She tensed. She was quiet a long moment, and he

did his best to hold her tenderly in his arms, stroking her in a way he hoped would soothe her.

Please let her trust me. Let her see that I care about her and that I only want her to have the wonderful life she deserves.

"Part of me understands your people. From your perspective, we're harming this world, a world you want to share as a home. So of course taking us over was the right thing to do. In your eyes, we should realize our mistakes and be grateful." She looked down at his chest as she spoke.

"But humans aren't like that, and honestly, if another race had conquered your people using the same rationale, I doubt you'd be grateful. I wonder if you'd have been part of your people's resistance to them?" Sef suspected Harper would have been a resistance fighter against a race that was intent on harming humans.

"I just want you to see things from my point of view, Sef. It's irrational, I know, but sometimes it's hard for us to see beyond our own little problems. You see an inhumane and barbaric practice like eating meat and shut it down. We see jobs lost, towns dying, and people suffering because of your good deeds."

"I didn't have a hand in those decisions. I can't say I would have done anything differently if that had been my assigned role, though. I want to be honest with you," Sef said.

"I know you do. And that's what I'm struggling with. Knowing that the man in front of me is a good man, that his people are good people, and trying to reconcile it with the bad things they've done trying to be good."

"Give me time—that's all I ask of you. Time to prove we're not the enemy."

"I don't...know. I want to, Sef, I do. Maybe I just need some time. I need to see your world, not be a prisoner here."

"I understand. I'll give you your freedom to leave the house, but you still must obey my commands. When I tell you not to do something, it is for your safety. Do you trust me on that?"

"Yes," she replied with certainty.

"Good." He kissed her temple, and she let out a relaxed sigh, her tense muscles finally giving way as she started to slip into sleep.

Silently, he told her with his body that she was a treasure, one he would keep safe. Tomorrow he would worry about how to save her brothers and how to find the Krinar who was willing to betray his people.

16

Harper lay in Sef's arms as dawn crested the horizon and filled the room with soft light.

Everything had changed.

She had decided after last night to surrender to Sef, to become his charl. Not because the sex last night had been literally out of this world, but because of the way he held her, the way she felt his love blossom inside her. He'd promised her freedom, promised her a good, happy life with him...if she could trust him. And she wanted to.

But she wasn't going to abandon her brothers either. She would talk with Mason and Liam today and tell them what she had learned about the Ks. She'd never hated them, but she hadn't understood them, not fully. Yet last night she'd spoken with Sarina and had realized that, in all the ways that mattered, the Krinar were just like humans. They weren't perfect, but they were unified in their desire to make Earth their home and to share it with humans. It wasn't about enslavement or extinction. The Krinar were waiting for humans to grow up and mature as a people, because right now they were on a path to destruction. It was like Sef had said—they wanted to be partners. She had to convince her brothers of this, but how?

Sef's sexy voice teased her. "You're starting the day with too many thoughts." She scooted over and propped her chin on his chest. He looked down the length of her body, his lips forming a seductive grin.

"I'm thinking about my brothers," she said.

Sef's body suddenly went rigid as his smile faded. She dropped her gaze to his chest and stroked a hand over his pectorals, but he didn't move, didn't speak, so she took a chance that he was open to listening.

"You are right. I don't really hate you. I like you too much. And I like your parents, and your brother and Bianca. You have a wonderful family who loves you and would do anything for you. I want to be one of those people for you too, but..." She placed her fingers over his lips when he tried to speak. "Just listen, okay?"

Sef gently curled his fingers around her wrist, his thumb massaging her skin, and he nodded.

"When I first came here, I wanted to resist you, to find a way to escape. But I don't want that anymore. I want to stay, but I have to save my brothers. They are *my* family. I feel about them the way you do about Soren. So what I'm asking is, will you please help me save them? I'm yours, and will be as long as you want me. All that I ask is for you to help save my family."

She held her breath, and her heart stuttered with uncertainty while she waited for him to say something.

He kissed the tips of her fingers, and his brown eyes burned gold. She thought she would miss those blue eyes from when he was Seth, but she was enraptured by his true eyes, those cinnamon-colored depths that always made her think of autumn.

"You are my family, Harper. That makes your brothers my family as well. I will do everything in my power to help."

Her eyes blurred with silly tears as she crushed her mouth to his, kissing him desperately. "Thank you."

It was another hour before they left the bed to go shower, and then another half hour in the tall, wide shower before they finally summoned the discipline to keep their hands off each other and get ready.

Harper dried her hair, then dressed in jeans and a loose pale-blue blouse that reminded her a bit of last night's dress. Memories of Sef ripping it apart made her flush all over again, even though she wasn't sure she could climax again so soon. She met Sef downstairs. He wore jeans and a white T-shirt that showed off his broad upper body. The man radiated raw, primal sexuality, especially when in jeans. Had he noticed how much he turned her on when he wore them? It made her want to climb him like a tree and wrap her legs around his waist and...

She stopped that train of thought before it got her in trouble.

"No K trousers?" she asked.

"I worked undercover so long that I grew to like denim." He chuckled. "You humans do a few things better than us, it seems." He held out a hand to her as he opened the front door. "You ready?"

She placed her hand in his and nodded. "Ready."

They walked toward the central part of the Kansas City Center. She and Sef held hands, something that drew a few looks, but nothing hostile, merely curious. She couldn't believe how accepting the Ks were of interspecies relationships. Humans would have been far more negative, possibly even hostile in their response.

"There aren't many human charls here. You'll have to forgive their curiosity," Sef murmured as they reached a white building with black windows.

"Why aren't there many charls here?"

He led her inside the two-story structure. "In part because it's a newer Center. Our older Centers have more of my people who have had interactions with yours."

"Which naturally lead to more *interactions*," Harper joked. But then her entire body went rigid as she saw that a dozen K males wearing cold white uniforms, just like the ones who'd captured her brothers, filled the room. Most were seated at desks and barely glanced at her.

"It's okay," Sef said as he led her past the men. There were dozens of transparent screens flashing with glowing alien text. Harper winced as her brain tried to make sense of the text, even though she knew it wasn't in English.

Sef paused, concern darkening his brown eyes and creating a furrow between his brows. "Are you okay?"

"Yeah, it's just a headache. I'm fine."

When he was satisfied that she was okay, he led her down the hall to a bay of elevators. The one they got in took them down to the basement one floor below. When the doors opened, she gasped. The hall was filled with dozens of cells. There were no bars, only thick-looking glass that separated her from those inside. There were a few people she recognized, but most she didn't.

Sef escorted her down the hall. "Your brothers are at the far end." She found her brothers sharing a cell. They had two full-size beds on opposite walls. Mason was lying on his back, throwing a tennis ball at the glass, catching it, and repeating the motion over and over. Liam was sitting on his bed, his face turned sideways to stare at the glass. He was the first to see her.

"Liam! Mason!" She rushed over to the glass,

pressing herself against it. Liam leaped up and ran to join her. Mason stared at her in shock, and the tennis ball smacked him in the chest. They both started speaking rapidly, but she couldn't hear them.

"Hang on." Sef lifted his hand up, staring at his palm. A second later the sound came through.

"Jesus, Harper! Are you okay? Did they arrest you too?" Liam demanded. His gaze cut to Sef beside her. "What the hell are you doing here with Ambassador Soren?" Liam tilted his head slightly, studying Sef.

"I'm not Ambassador Soren. Look again, more closely," Sef encouraged calmly as he moved toward the glass wall.

"No...no way," Mason growled. "It's Seth. From the bar. Picture him blond and blue-eyed." He smacked a balled fist against the glass. "He's a fucking K!"

"You lying mother fu—" Liam started to snarl.

"Liam! Mason! Stop that!" Harper snapped. "Just calm down, okay?"

"Calm down? We're in *prison* because of him!" said Mason.

"And if he's touched you in any way...," Liam warned.

"Oh, grow up." She turned to Sef. "Is there any way I can go in and talk to them?"

Sef nodded, did something with his palm controller, and pointed at the glass. "You can now walk through it."

"Okay." Heart pounding, she stepped through the glass. She closed her eyes, and cool tingling sensations covered her body for a few seconds until she passed completely through the glass. It felt like walking through mist. Her brothers both stepped back warily.

"Whoa," Mason said, his eyes wide.

"Yeah," she laughed. "Their technology is amazing."

"Of course it is. How do you think they took over the planet so easily?" Mason grumbled as he shot Sef a dark glare. "Might as well be magic."

"Not really," said Harper. "The fundamental principles seem pretty straightforward. It's the application that makes all their tech seem magical."

"I'll come back in a few minutes." Sef gave her a small nod and gave them some privacy.

The moment he was gone, her brothers crushed her in a fierce embrace. She smacked on Mason's back and gasped for breath.

"Sorry. We've been worried sick about you, kiddo." Mason released her, and she had a minute to look them over. "We didn't know if you'd gotten caught up in all this as a bystander."

"They don't seem to be about due process," Liam added. "So who knows what rights you have in their view?"

They were still wearing the same clothes from the night they'd been captured, and they were both sporting scruff, which meant they hadn't been allowed to shave.

"How badly are they treating you?" she asked them.

Liam said, "I wish I could say the aliens are grade A assholes, but we haven't been mistreated at all."

"What? But your clothes—you haven't changed."

"We have. They used some fancy device called a fabricator to replicate the exact clothes we were wearing." Mason pointed to a wall and spoke. "Shirts, please."

A drawer opened up from a previously blank wall, and she saw several folded shirts in the same color he currently wore resting inside.

"These little Roombas are stealing our dirty clothes when we drop them on the ground. Damn thing scared the shit out of me the first time it came out of the wall." Mason and Liam chuckled a bit. You had to find humor where you could at times like this.

"Where have they been keeping you?" Liam asked. "Another cell down the hall?"

"No, I've been staying elsewhere. I'm not a prisoner. Not really."

Liam crossed his arms, frowning. "What does that mean?"

"I'm staying with Sef. That's his real name, by the way—Sef with an *f*, not Seth with a *th*."

"You're *staying* with him? Harper, please tell me

you didn't do something stupid," Mason hissed, and Liam punched him hard in the arm.

"I didn't do anything stupid. What I *did* do was save both your asses. Rebels deemed a threat to humans and Krinar are rehabilitated. You know what that means around here? They erase most of your recent memories."

"What?" Liam's face was as white as alabaster, and Mason cursed violently.

"I bought you both time. If you listen to me, Sef and I could stop that from happening."

"How?" Liam sat back down on his bed, his face gravely serious. Mason paced the length of their cell.

"You have to trust me. Trust me when I tell you that the situation between us and the Ks isn't so black-and-white, good and evil. The Krinar are not the villains we thought they were. They do view us as equals in more ways than we realize. They want to share our planet. I know they can seem brutal at times, but they are also compassionate. Yes, they are stronger and faster, but they have never attacked first, only in defense. They want to trust us. But we have to trust them first." She knew she wasn't explaining this right. She had so little time to get through to them.

"They took over our *planet*, Harper," Liam reminded her.

"They didn't kill us. They didn't enslave us. They let life go on. They built these Centers because they're afraid. They fear we will attack them when they protect us from our own destructive tendencies. It took me a while to understand, but I do now. I get it. They are trying to save this planet, because they need it as a home as much as we do. But sometimes their changes aren't painless, and people have wanted to blame them for taking charge. It's like when you see someone stuck on a railroad track and the train's coming. The Ks are pushing us forcibly but necessarily out of the path of danger. I trust them."

"How can you?" Mason snapped. "How can you *side* with them? Mom and Dad are dead because of them."

"Mom and Dad died because some human idiot wanted to blow up that bridge. A *human* killed them. And that attack was completely unnecessary, because the Ks arrived in flying ships. Why would they care about a human bridge when they wouldn't use it? It's time for us to look in the mirror as a race and see this. *We* are half of the problem."

Neither of her brothers spoke for a long moment. Then Liam stood, his shoulders drooping as he released a weary sigh.

"What's it going to take to get us out of here and back to working at our bar?"

"Does this mean you trust me?" She was too afraid to hope. Her brothers could both be so stubborn.

"I dunno. But I think you're right about one thing— we don't have all the information. Not the way we believed we did. Mom always said that the most important things in life often require you to take a leap of faith. So, I'll leap." Liam looked toward Mason, whose mouth was curved in a heavy scowl.

"Mason?" Liam prompted.

"Seriously?" He cursed. "Fine, whatever. I'll do what I have to, even if it means playing nice with E.T. over there." He jerked his head in the direction Sef had gone.

Liam hugged Harper. "Just tell us what we have to do."

"I will. When Sef returns, we'll—"

Whatever she'd been about to say was forgotten as an explosion rocked the walls around them. The lights died, and the force of the blast sent her, Liam, and Mason flying into the wall. Pain was the only thing she registered as she blacked out.

———

SEF STOPPED IN FRONT OF A CELL CONTAINING A different prisoner from the King's Bar raid. Mitch Davis stared at him as he approached. Sef turned on the communication system.

"Mr. Davis," he said.

Davis just flipped him the middle finger. Though he knew what the hand gesture meant, it made no impact whatsoever.

"Prior to your detainment, you were recorded saying that you had a contact in the Center. One of my people was working with you. I want a name."

Mitch laughed. "I'm not telling you anything. Not even if you torture me."

"I have no desire to torture you. Even if you give humans as a whole a bad name." Sef crossed his arms over his chest. "You know what happens when we deal with a threat?"

"Yeah, I do. The ones you don't kill just disappear. Doesn't take a genius to know you kill them too," Mitch sneered.

Sef smiled this time. "I'm sure that's what you want, to be seen as a martyr for your cause. No. We erase your memories, all the ones that make you, well, *you*. You become a blank slate, and we teach you what you should have known from the start. We don't want to hurt you, but if you're endangering innocent lives, human and Krinar, we won't stand for it. So ask yourself, Mr. Davis, is it worth it?"

Mitch stared at him in dawning horror. "So I would be some Krinar puppet?"

Sef wouldn't call it that. Some former rebels had now become influential and positive people in society. They worked with the Krinar rather than against them, but he sensed this man's fear now and needed answers, so if he had to lie to get them, then so be it.

"Yes. You would be our puppet, and we would pull

the strings. Your fellow rebels would consider you a traitor."

Mitch swallowed hard, his bravado fading. "And if I talk?"

"Then we won't wipe your mind." That was also a lie.

This man wasn't like the other rebels. They had been interviewed and psychologically assessed, and they had been deemed able to return to their lives in Lawrence without rehabilitation. Their houses would be watched for a year or so to make sure they didn't continue with rebel activities, but he doubted they would. Mitch, on the other hand, was a clear and present danger to humans and the Krinar.

"Fine, the K who contacted me was—"

A deafening explosion directly behind Mitch's bed hit Sef so hard he was thrown back against the opposite wall. Fire blossomed in the cell as the lights in the prison section winked out. He groaned and picked himself up off the ground. His ears rang as he struggled to make sense of what had just happened.

Mitch's body had been blown in half and lay about a dozen feet away. The fire licking the crumbled wall of the cell illuminated his smoldering corpse. Someone had wanted Mitch dead before he could talk. And given the timing, someone had hacked into the system to listen to see if Mitch would spill his secrets.

Screams came from all around him. He tried to

access the systems, and he started opening cell doors as per evacuation protocol. Humans stumbled out of the hall.

"Harper!" He rushed past them toward the cell she was in.

"What's going on?" a human demanded as he followed Sef.

"Someone just killed Mitch Davis," Sef told him. "One of my people has betrayed us. It's not safe for you to evacuate just yet. There may be another attack. Follow me and you will be safe."

"Trust a K?" the man snarled. "No way in hell."

"Trust him," a human woman said. "Harper King was with him. She wouldn't be if she didn't trust him."

The remaining humans followed him as he reached the cell. The glass front of their cell was shattered like all the rest. Liam and Mason were getting to their feet. Harper was down, blood trickling from her lips. Sef rushed over and lifted her into his arms.

"Liam, Mason, and the rest of you, come with me." He got to the elevator, which thankfully still worked. The bomb in Mitch's cell had been the only one in the building, but it had caused damage to all the other cells. It wasn't safe for the other detainees to stay there amid the damage. Everyone climbed inside the elevator, cramming against each other, but Sef had only one care. His charl. The moment the elevator doors opened on the main floor, a fleet of guardians were there, weapons raised. One male stepped forward.

"Sef? What happened? The feed went dark, and there was an explosion."

"Davis was assassinated, Trevlin," Sef announced. "Someone planted an explosive device down there."

"Not just here—several places along the Center's border walls were destroyed," Trevlin added grimly as he and the other guardians lowered their weapons. "The timing can't be a coincidence."

"We need medical aid," Liam said. "My sister's hurt."

Trevlin turned to his desk nearby and tossed Sef a jansha, a Krinar healing device.

"See to the other humans, Trevlin, and see to it they remain under observation. The King brothers will remain in my custody." Sef placed Harper on the ground and began scanning the jansha over her head and then the rest of her, getting a reading of her injuries. Then the device began to heal her, first the small cuts, then knitting together a fractured set of ribs and a broken nose, but it was the internal bleeding that concerned him most. He called for Trevlin to bring in a nanocytes injector. Trevlin brought it to him and Sef raised it to Harper's chest, but Mason grabbed his arm.

"What is that?"

Sef shook the arm off like it was that of a child. "It will save her life, that's what it is." There wasn't time to have a philosophical discussion of the ramifications of giving Harper what humans would equate to immortality.

"Fine—do what you have to."

Sef injected the nanocytes, and then he cradled her in his arms as the nanocytes went to work on repairing her damaged organs.

Liam and Mason stayed on either side of him, neither one daring to look away.

When Harper's breathing became steady, Sef finally let out his own breath.

"Is she going to make it?" Liam asked.

"Yes." He lowered his head to hers, touching his forehead to Harper's. "You are safe now, Queenie. Now and always," he whispered. Sef would find out who had betrayed his people and put a stop to it. *Forever*. No one would ever hurt his mate again.

———

THE NEXT MORNING, SEF HELD HARPER'S HAND WHERE she lay in a bed in their healing facilities. She was still unconscious as the nanocytes worked through her system.

"So what exactly was that?" Liam asked. Both he and Mason had stayed by her side the entire night.

"The nanocytes will work on her injuries and return her to peak health." He explained how Harper would never age now. Mason and Liam took the news better than he'd expected. For a long moment, he had expected them to be furious. But instead, Liam nodded slowly in acceptance.

"She won't be able to die, like Mom and Dad. I guess I'm okay with that."

"Me too," Mason agreed. "It will suck that we'll get old, but I'd do anything to keep her alive and healthy."

Sef let go of Harper's hand and faced them both. All three of them had been in this room too damn long.

"If you really want to do what's best for your sister, I have an idea."

"We're listening," Liam said, and he crossed his arms and waited for Sef to continue.

"Those who were part of your rebel cell are not going to be reeducated, but you, as their leaders, are another matter. However, I told Harper that I can keep you from being reeducated if I could convince you about my people's true intentions and why we have done what we have. I want you to understand us, our technology, our history, our lives. Will you give me a few days to show you life here in the Center?"

"Not unless you listen to our grievances as well," Liam said. "And not just listen, actually have a plan about what to do about them. You lived in Lawrence long enough to see that the town was dying. And you know why. It was your rules that killed our city's lifeblood, without any regard for the fallout. If I'm going to give understanding your people a shot, then I want you to at least think about how you can help towns like Lawrence survive."

"That's fair," Sef agreed. "And I promise I'll answer as many questions as I can."

"You mean you won't tell us everything." Mason's shrewd observation wasn't unexpected.

"No. Because some information could be used to hurt my people and other humans. Like the nanocytes. If knowledge of them got out to the wrong people, you'd have dictators doing just about anything to obtain them and then living forever. That's just one example of the sort of nightmare you'd face. It's our intention to have your people learn over time, as you learn to trust us and learn to use what we give you with good judgment. My people were violent and hungry for power long ago, but we've finally outgrown that, for the most part. You are developing much faster than we expected. In some ways that is good, but it also comes with its own share of risks."

Mason and Liam shared a look, and then Liam spoke. "Okay, I guess we can agree to that."

"Good. If you still can't trust me when we are done...well, I'll do my best to protect you, but the Krinar Council will insist that you be dealt with."

"Jeez, no pressure," Mason said, though there was a hint of humor to it.

Sef looked down at Harper's sleeping form, wishing he could tell her that he was sticking to his promise and fighting for her family as if they were his own.

Maybe this would work.

17

Everything was white. That was why Harper thought she was dead. That and the fact that her brothers and Sef were all peering down at her in common concern rather than fighting each other.

"She's still pale, but she looks better," Liam said.

Sef nodded in agreement. "There was much to repair internally." Sef leaned over her and brushed the back of his hand over her cheek.

"I'm not dead?" she asked. Her throat ached, and her limbs were weak.

"No, you're not," Mason laughed. "Why would you think that?"

"Because...because you aren't fighting..." A horrible thought occurred to her. Had their memories been wiped after all? Sef had promised her he would find a way to save them. Her chest tightened, and her hands balled into fists. She didn't want to believe it.

"We aren't fighting because we listened to you," Liam said. "You've been in a 'special low-cognitive state to facilitate physical repairs,' as the Ks put it."

"Or to put it more simply," Mason added, "a medically induced coma."

She tried to sit up, but Mason urged her back down on the bed. "How long was I out?"

"Four days," Sef murmured, his eyes searching hers.

"Oh God..."

"It's okay," Liam assured her. "Sef had the other Ks show us around the Center, and we got a chance to see what they are like up close. It's not what I thought. You were right about them, and about us," he admitted, his eyes downcast.

"Yeah, I think it's pretty cool after all," Mason added. "Driana is this super-smoking-hot K, and she's been helping to heal you. She had a look at your brain and said she could fix you."

Harper's head was still a little fuzzy. "Fix me...you mean, my dyslexia?"

"Yeah. If you want to fix it, that is." Mason chewed his lip, clearly realizing he had made a mistake in suggesting it.

"I'm not broken," she insisted, her body tightening with shame.

Sef eased down on the bed beside her. "It's not about being broken. There is a way to correct your neural pathways so that you don't have those headaches when you try to read. Humans who need glasses don't feel broken. The choice is entirely up to you, of course. You are mine no matter what, and I love you just the way you are."

His words brought on fresh tears. "Can I have some time to think about it? I'd need to know more about what's involved." She wanted to be sure it wouldn't affect anything else about her in the process.

"You have all the time in the world." Sef's face was so open, so unshuttered. She could read a dozen emotions now in his features, all of them full of hope and affection.

Had she really done the right thing? Had she saved her brothers from their quest for vengeance? Had her heart finally found its other half? She was afraid to believe it, but one thing was certain—there was no going back, only forward from now on.

Two hours later, Sef escorted her home from the medical center. When she stepped inside, she gasped. Pictures of her family and other items from her apartment were all there, neatly placed on shelves and walls as if she had decorated the house herself.

"I hope you don't mind," Sef said. "My mother was a bit overexcited to settle you in, and she convinced me to decorate it for you. She said my home was barren and unwelcoming for my mate. So I put everything up last night, and I may have covered many surfaces with vases of wild blooms from the flowers of my home world. I wanted you to come home to color and life. It was the only time I could bear to leave your side."

"You stayed with me?" She couldn't believe it. "You weren't out hunting for whoever blew up the detention center?" Back in Lawrence, he had put his work first, to the point of betraying her and breaking her heart. Had he changed?

"Yes. I stayed with you the entire time. I entrusted Trevlin to track down the male who betrayed us."

"Did you catch him?"

Sef nodded. "Yes. His name is Uther. I don't know him. He came from Krina on one of our recent transports. His motivations in helping the resistance were far from selfless. He intended to gain power for himself here on Earth. The bombing that was being planned was a ruse—not to expose us, but to break into one of our research labs to steal some new technology to use for his own personal gain. He will face judgment before our Council. The humans arrested with your brothers have been unharmed, aside from Mitch Davis, who died in the explosion. Their memories will remain intact, and they have been returned home. We gave them access to our world here, and like your brothers, they changed their minds about us."

Harper turned to face Sef, stepping into his open

arms. She took in his rich scent as he held her, one that reminded her of the passion shared between them.

"Harper, I must tell you something." Sef pulled back so that she could see his troubled expression.

"What is it?"

"I was wrong to force you to come here with me. I stole you away from your life in Lawrence. I..." He paused, stark pain in his eyes. "I am offering you the freedom now to leave. I should've offered it to you the first time, but I was so blinded by my desire for you that I was wrong."

She stepped back, his hands dropping from her body. "Wait, what? You don't want me now? What are you saying?"

"I will *always* want you, more than my own life," Sef vowed. "What I am trying to say is that I release you from your promise. Your brothers are safe, and you no longer have to stay with me to protect them."

Harper was quiet a long moment, searching her heart for what she truly wanted for her future.

"Do you love me?" she asked at last.

Sef smiled. "It may have taken eight thousand years, but yes, I have found love. I cannot imagine a world without you in it. You own me, Harper. You own my heart." He looked down at his boots and chuckled. "I thought fear was at the heart of love and that was what made it so dangerous. But now I realize that only courage and compassion dwell at its core. I am honored by the days you have given me, and even if you choose to leave, I will never regret loving you, not for a second."

Harper bit her lip, wanting so desperately to kiss him, but she extended her hand to him first.

"From this moment on, there will be no secrets, no more games or power plays between us. You won't ever use anything as leverage against me again. Swear it."

He caught her hand, lacing their fingers. "No more."

"And I'll stay with you, wherever you go. Forever."

He tugged her to his chest. "You should know then that could be a *very* long time."

"What?"

"We have forever ahead of us now. The nanocytes used to save you have seen to that. You won't grow old, and you won't die."

She struggled to process that, her mind reeling. "But what about Liam and Mason?" She could think of another dozen people she didn't want to lose to old age while she remained forever young, but she couldn't live without her brothers. They mattered most, if she had to make impossible choices.

"We can petition the Council for them to receive nanocytes. It's a lengthy process, but we could argue that it will help build bridges between our people. But if they happen to become charls to any of my kind in the meantime, they will be granted them, just as you have."

Harper smiled. "I guess I'm going to have to play matchmaker then, huh?"

"I've taken the liberty of getting started. I've had a number of single females I know show them around the Center, and several have shown great interest in them. I think it's safe to say it's only a matter of time before they settle down."

He rubbed his cheek against the crown of her hair, and she tilted her head to feather her lips along his jaw as she reached for his mouth. They kissed, and their embrace tightened, their love carrying the heat of a newborn star and the strength of the tides.

Falling in love was easy, but loving someone who had broken her heart and learning to trust him a second time—*that* had taken every ounce of her courage. And she did trust Sef now, because she saw that her Krinar had a code of honor, a code that extended to those he loved. She could give Sef every bit of herself because he would never break that Krinar code of love and loyalty.

She brushed her fingertips along the back of his neck as they kissed. Once their mouths parted, she gazed up at him.

"Ready to be a father yet?" she asked.

His eyes widened. "But that's not possible."

"I know, but you said it would be eventually, and I want lots of practice beforehand."

Sef's eyes gleamed with sensual hunger. "I see. Then we should practice right now."

He scooped her up in his arms and raced upstairs, laughing the entire way.

EPILOGUE

T*wo months later*
Harper peered at the tablet in front of her that explained the complex engineering system of a new spacecraft. Every letter and number stayed perfectly still, and her head was ache free. It had taken only two days for her to decide to let the Ks adjust the neural pathways in her brain, and now literally an entire universe of possibilities had opened up for her.

While many of the mechanical elements of their technology were close to what she had predicted, their understanding of physics was far more advanced, which left the science of things like their power sources a mystery to her...for now. She was learning new things at a wild rate, partly thanks to the nanocytes keeping her body and mind at an optimal condition.

She had started working on a new design for a small flying vessel with a little help from a Krinar engineer named Korum, who Sef said was one of their best technological experts.

Her life had become wonderful in the most unexpected ways. Both of her brothers had become charls to Ks of their own and seemed quite content with that. Liam and Mason's mates, Pria and Driana, were both fascinated with humanity. Driana was a biologist who would be teaching at Princeton that fall. Her daily commute between Kansas and New Jersey was possible thanks to Krinar flight technology. Pria was a doctor, or healer, as they put it, and she planned to open a clinic in Lawrence to work with human patients. It never ceased to amaze her that her brothers had managed to win over two intelligent females as mates. Who'd have thunk it?

Her brothers were leaving the Center tomorrow to return to Lawrence with their cheren to get back to work at King's Bar. It had taken some getting used to by the local townsfolk, but the pub was now a regular attraction for anyone who was curious about the Krinar. Pria and Driana had started to work with the Krinar Council on solutions for human towns suffering from an economic loss after the invasion. Plans for new ways to revitalize were already in order. Harper had sold her auto shop to Ruby, who had hired out several local mechanics in addition to Jeff and

Alan, so it was doing well. Sef had given Harper the freedom to do what she loved with the man she loved, and that was what she was doing at exactly that moment.

She looked over at Sef, who sat beside her at the large desk as he pored over her old blueprints, double-checking the math of her equations. He'd left the guardians and taken up engineering again. His first task had been to help her complete her original designs, as a means of helping her learn the fundamentals of Krinar technology.

Harper couldn't help but remember how she'd first seen him in the bar, blond-haired and blue-eyed, and how so much had changed when she saw the real Sef, with dark hair and dark eyes. And yet so much of him was the same.

The man he was, the man who had believed in her even when she'd doubted herself, the man who'd known they were meant to be together—that man had never changed. He'd fought for what he believed was right, and while he might have been a bit foolish to blackmail her to come with him to the K Center as his charl, he hadn't taken advantage of her, had given her the time and space to realize that he was in fact what she wanted. He'd given her the chance to walk away, to have the freedom she thought she needed. But being with him now, like this? This was the truest freedom she'd ever experienced.

"I love you, you know," she whispered.

His brown eyes met hers. "I know. I love you too." He reached over and placed a palm on her thigh, stroking her in a way he knew would have her ready for him in less than a minute.

The doorbell chimed, and Sef grinned. "But you are going to love me even more in a minute, I hope." He stood and pulled her to her feet. "We have a very important guest."

Mystified, she followed him downstairs and to the front door.

"Please try not to be alarmed," he said as he opened the door.

A lovely young brunette woman stood on the porch, and a tall, darkly handsome man was right behind her, his hands on her shoulders. It took her a second to realize that the woman was human.

"Hello, Harper," the woman said, her face red as she smiled in embarrassment.

Harper looked at the woman, a strange sense of déjà vu tugging at her mind. Her breath caught in her throat as she stared at the woman who seemed more and more familiar by the second.

"Harper, honey...it's me." That voice. That tone. The tone was so hauntingly familiar, as though she'd heard someone saying her name like that a thousand times. Because she had. Harper stared into the woman's eyes, searching for answers, and then she realized what was so odd. The woman had *her* eyes, the same slightly almond-shaped creamy brown eyes.

No...there is no way...but...

Harper cleared her throat, trying to speak past the sudden lump that had formed there.

"Mom?" It was impossible, yet somehow it was true. Pamela King stood there, looking as young as Harper was at that moment.

"Yes, honey, I've..." The young woman's smile suddenly wavered as she choked back a sob. "I wanted so badly to see you, to come and find you after Zane saved me, but I couldn't go back, not like this."

Wiping away tears, Harper looked to the handsome male behind the young woman who was and yet couldn't be her mother.

"I rescued your mother from the river five years ago. I failed to reach your father in time. I tended to your mother, healing her of her injuries by using the nanocytes, and I fell in love with her. I begged her to become my charl. It was why she couldn't go home to see you. Humans who are not charls are not allowed to know about our nanotechnology."

Harper's head felt light as she stared at the woman who looked to be around her age, yet she knew it was her mother. "Sef? How...?"

"While you were recovering, I searched for information about your mother, hoping to give you some peace by knowing her fate. I heard from Arus only yesterday that she was still alive. I contacted Zane last night to see if he would bring her to see you. I didn't tell you sooner because I was afraid to let you down if they didn't come." Concern flashed across his features. "Are you upset?"

"Upset?" she echoed faintly. "You brought my mother back to me, Sef. You did the impossible. If it was possible to love you any more than I already do, I would." She placed a hand on his cheek and smiled, then flung herself at her mother, hugging her so hard they both gasped for air, before they both broke out into laughter.

It took a while to catch her mother up on everything that had happened to her and her brothers. She gasped at how close they had come to having their memories wiped, and the explosion in the prison, but she sighed in relief once she learned everything had worked out so well.

"And they fixed your dyslexia?" Her mother stared at her, tears in her eyes.

"Yes. I was nervous to at first. I didn't want people to think something was wrong with me. But the pain was bad, and I knew this could work, and I wanted...I wanted to be the best version of myself possible. Once I came to accept that I wasn't fixing something inside me that was broken, I was merely accepting that the advanced science could help me, it all became so clear."

"Honey, that's incredible." Her mother hugged her again, and Harper marveled at how strange it felt to have her mother back, yet physically the same age as her. In fact, she looked to be around the age she would have been when she'd given birth to Liam.

"Mom...do you miss Dad?" Harper whispered, even though she suspected Zane could hear, but she had to know.

"Of course, honey. Every day. But if there's one thing I've learned in life, it's this. You have moments where the world has given you everything—a husband you love, a family you love, a life you love. But that moment doesn't always last. Some beautiful wonders in life are not endless, no matter how brilliant they may be. I loved your father with all my heart, but I lost him that day the bridge collapsed. Once my heart healed, I realized that despite the pain I'd suffered, my life wasn't over. I'd been given a second chance with Zane, and I wasn't going to let that chance slip away. I don't think Jim would have minded. And if the situation had been reversed, I would have wanted him to find his second chance too."

Harper's heart swelled with emotion. Sef was her second chance. Xander had broken her heart, and Sef had shown her how to put the pieces back together. She didn't need a man to complete her, but Sef's love had shown her that she deserved to love herself and be proud of who she was. She couldn't help but fall hopelessly in love with a man like that, even if he was from another world.

"I'm so glad you and the boys are with the Krinar now. Perhaps we can be a family again. All of us." Her mother looked to Zane, who smiled back. Harper didn't miss the look of open adoration on Zane's face. Her mother was truly loved, and that was all that mattered.

Hours later, after her mother and Zane had left with the promise of meeting again the next day, Harper took Sef's hand and led him to their bedroom. She pushed him to lie back on the bed and crawled in beside him.

"Linda, lights off please," she ordered. The lights around them dropped into almost pitch blackness.

"Harper, what are you—?"

"Shh." She silenced him with a kiss before she spoke again. "Linda, show us the stars." That's exactly what the central core system did. It beamed a vast virtual blanket of stars and galaxies over their heads.

"Make love to me beneath the stars," she said.

Sef rolled her beneath him, and they came together with fire and passion. Harper knew then that Sef had been right all along. There was hope for Earth, so long as humans and the Krinar could come together like this, with undying love, loyalty, and compassion.

. . .

THANK YOU SO MUCH FOR READING *THE KRINAR CODE*! If you haven't read Soren and Bianca's story yet, keep reading for a 3 chapter sneak peek of *The Krinar Code* by Lauren Smith!

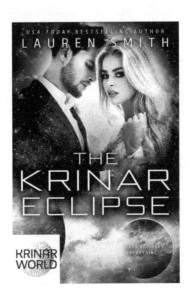

BEFORE YOU TURN THE PAGE...

The best way to know when a new book is released is to do one or all of the following:

Join my Newsletter: https://bit.ly/2Y65kF5

Follow Me on BookBub: https://www.bookbub.com/authors/emma-castle

Join my Facebook Exclusive Reader Group called Emma Castle's Crew: https://www.facebook.com/groups/429283600812685/

Now...turn the page to see how Soren seduces Bianca in *The Krinar Eclipse*!

THE KRINAR ECLIPSE BY LAUREN SMITH

PROLOGUE

F*ive years ago*
     Bianca's sweet sixteenth birthday should have been celebrated with a new car in the driveway with a pretty bow on it, *not* with an imminent alien invasion. Instead of Bianca rushing out the door, shiny new keys in hand, two Secret Service agents rushed into her bedroom and hustled her into the hallway toward her father's room.

"We have secured Hummingbird. Repeat, we have secured Hummingbird," one agent said into his ear mic. The two armed men trapped her near the back wall of her father's bedroom, shielding her with their bodies.

"Bianca?" Her father rushed over to her, his own security detail flanking him. "Are you all right?"

"I'm fine..." Her voice shook as she looked around the room. "What's going on?"

"A ship has appeared in orbit, just outside our atmosphere."

"A ship? What do you mean, *a ship*?" Bianca stared at her father's ashen face. There was really only one possible answer, but she had to hear it for herself.

"A spaceship."

Bianca would have laughed if it wasn't for the looks on the faces of the men around her. No one was joking.

"You mean...like aliens?" Her heart raced so violently in her chest that it hurt. She struggled to process what was happening.

"Yes, we—" Her father's words were cut off as a man materialized in front of them in the center of the room with a flash of light. The man—or alien, presumably—looked straight at her father.

The Secret Service agents drew their guns on the sudden intruder. Bianca just stared at the man—who looked human, yet was somehow too *perfect* to be human—as he spoke to her father. This was no thin green specter with oval-shaped black eyes who'd dropped to Earth in a beam of light from a flying saucer. This...*creature* looked more like he'd stepped off the cover of a fashion magazine. It didn't make sense. Why would aliens look so human?

His speech was slow and measured, with a hint of an accent she'd never heard before. Her stomach knotted, and her body flushed with a rush of heat as she stared, bewitched, at the beautiful man before her. She was only sixteen, but her hormones were already raging. She knew a sexy man when she saw one, and this one was *beyond* sexy.

"President Wells, I know you spoke to Arus, one of my kind, a few minutes ago, and he made it clear that we, the Krinar people, are no threat to you." The man was tall, too tall, with russet hair and brown eyes that seemed to flash a tawny gold every few seconds. There was something terrifying and fascinating about him that made it impossible to look away.

"I did speak with Arus. Who are you?" her father asked.

"My name is Soren. Arus has assigned me the role of..." Soren paused, his lips twitching in a near smile as he seemed to search for the right word. "Ambassador."

Bianca strained to see over the shoulders of her Secret Service detail. They wedged her between their two large bodies and the wall, smothering her with fear and panic as wild thoughts of a hundred alien invasion movies swarmed in her head. There was a soft rumble to the man's deep voice that seemed to put her at ease as her instincts screamed that nothing was calming about facing off with an alien.

In fact, she knew without a doubt that something was terribly wrong, because she should have been screaming and trying to escape...yet her voice wouldn't work. She was rooted to the spot in horror and fascination.

"I am to represent the needs of the Krinar people on Earth. Any issues that arise will be dealt with by me." The man crossed the room and seated himself in an armchair, the one her father liked to sit in at night and smoke a cigar when he had the chance.

"You have been poor custodians of such a precious planet. You have ruined it. We are here to fix what we can, and you will be thankful for the intervention."

This man...alien...who called himself Soren, simply leaned back, hands on the armrests in a picture of complete ease, watching them without fear. His casual, carefree attitude warned Bianca that whoever these Krinar were, they weren't afraid of humans at all. That meant they had power, and lots of it.

Soren cleared his throat politely and continued. "I assume you don't mind if I procure a residence close to yours. It will give me time to acclimate. I have not set foot on your world in more than five thousand years." Soren chuckled. "Much has changed."

Her father seemed to recover himself. "Five *thousand* years?"

"Yes. I was checking in on your progress. Egypt was the center of advanced technology. They were quite gifted."

"Our progress?" Bianca spoke up, only to have one

of her agents mutter a curse and try to remove her from the room. But she dug in her heels.

"Stop. Leave her be." Soren's commanding voice stilled the agent gripping her, and his hold loosened. "Who is this?" Soren seemed to notice her for the first time. Her father stepped between her and the Krinar man.

"My daughter, Bianca. She normally wouldn't be in here, but your little magic act has my security team noticeably concerned, and they thought it best to bring her to my room." Her father waved at the agents hovering near him and Bianca.

Soren raised a dark brow, studying Bianca. There was a knowing look in his gaze, as though he could read every thought she'd ever had. There would be no keeping secrets from him. A sudden shiver rippled down her spine at the thought of feeling so powerless against a man like him.

"Today is your birthday?" he asked as he looked down at his palm. Had he written notes on it, like she did when she was worried she'd forget something? The idea of a powerful alien needing to scribble down notes on his hand struck her as both funny and bizarre.

"Y–yes," she replied. He then moved a few steps closer, and she saw that his palm was empty of notes. What had he been looking at? And how had he known about her birthday?

"Happy birthday, then. Sixteen is an important year in a human's life, I'm told." Soren smiled and turned his focus back to her father, having lost all interest in her.

"Now, Mr. President, it's time we talked peace terms in order to prevent millions of innocent deaths." He rose with confidence and preternatural grace from the armchair and came face-to-face with her father. "Here's how Earth is going to surrender to Krinar control." Bianca felt like she'd swallowed her tongue whole as she stared at the gorgeous, scary-as-hell man who had just announced that his people were not only invading, but had already won. All she could think was that he reminded her of a leopard she'd once seen in a zoo. So close against the glass, golden eyes hungry with dark intent...

A predator.

Bianca opened her mouth to scream, but no sound came out.

CHAPTER 1

Bianca bolted upright in bed, heart smashing against her ribs. Her roommate, Claudia, stared at her. The other girl flipped on the light between their two beds and watched her nervously.

"You'd have that dream about *him* again?" Claudia asked, her blue eyes wide. Bianca nodded. Mortification deadened her limbs as she realized she'd woken up her roommate with her screaming.

Today was her twenty-first birthday, and like clockwork, the nightmares had come back. K-Day. The day the Krinar had arrived and taken over. Everything that Bianca had believed about her life and even Earth itself had been turned on its head once the Krinar had made some announcements to the world.

Thousands of years ago, the Krinar had modified existing life on Earth to become compatible with and originate from Krinar-based DNA in order to create humans. Humans were nothing more than ants in an ant farm to them. She couldn't help but fear the day one of those Ks would give their little ant farm called Earth a mighty shake.

"I'm just glad the agents have the night off," she muttered.

Claudia nodded. The first couple of times she'd had nightmares, her agents had rushed into the room, guns drawn. Claudia had almost asked for a new room-mate from Princeton's college housing. But Bianca had convinced her not to, and they'd told the agents they had to take nights off. All that really meant was that they took up a post in an SUV parked in front of the dorm. At least from there they couldn't hear her scream. She had to wear her panic button around her wrist at all times. She was glad the White House tech team had been able to make it so small. Embedded in a leather bracelet, it looked more like a fashion acces-sory than a personal security device.

Claudia slipped out of bed and headed into their shared bathroom. "Want me to get you some water?"

Bianca rubbed her eyes and drew in a slow breath. She wasn't sixteen anymore. She was finishing her final year at Princeton. She wasn't helpless, wasn't trapped beneath Soren's predatory gaze. Yet even after five years, thoughts of him, the first Krinar she'd ever seen, wouldn't go away. Her stomach knotted, and she suppressed a moan as she fought off the wave of nausea that came with it.

Flashes of memories, slices of that moment always came back. Predatory golden-brown eyes that threatened to swallow her whole. After she had seen him, heard his calm demands all those years ago, she had been escorted to her room and kept under lock and key while her father, the president, had spoken with him for the next four hours about the future of mankind and how best to protect the American people from panicking. It was why her father had been reelected by a landslide. He'd kept the Great Panic that had followed the invasion limited. America and the other major countries of the world had kept the confusion and casualties as low as possible.

"Here." Claudia held out a glass of water, which Bianca gratefully accepted. She curled her fingers around the glass and drank deeply. There was something purifying about water after she had nightmares, as it washed away the metallic tang in her mouth that always accompanied her nightmares.

"It's been five years. You'd think you'd have adjusted by now," said Claudia.

"You weren't there," said Bianca. "I didn't have any kind of warning to cushion the blow like most people did."

"I can't believe you were up close to *Soren*, on K-Day no less." Claudia sat cross-legged on the bed and ran her fingers through her red hair. Now she was awake and wanted to talk, but Bianca just wanted to curl up in a ball and try to make the dreams go away. Ever since K-Day, she had seen Soren *everywhere*. His arrogant, handsome face appeared on TV interviews, magazine covers, and internet articles.

The Krinar male was handsome, she could acknowledge that, but she hated him. Hated him because he'd been the first person to really look at her and then just as quickly dismiss her. She was one small, meaningless part of a race his had experimented on over eons. Just a kid. But now? She wasn't a kid anymore. What would he think of her if they came face-to-face again after all these years? She hoped she'd never know. Going to college had helped her avoid most of her father's political functions. Her mother had died before he took office, and Bianca had taken the unofficial position of her father's "plus one" to every gala and state dinner. But after the Krinar invaded, she'd been invited to fewer and fewer of those events for safety reasons, which was fine by her.

"Soren's so intimidating," Claudia continued. "But in kind of a *hot* way, you know? Like if he kissed you, you would just melt through the floor. My sister's friend went to an X-club, you know. And wow, she can't even talk about it. She gets this dazed, swoony look on her face."

That had Bianca sitting up. "Your sister knows someone who went to an X-club?"

Those were Krinar sex clubs. Well, that's what the news called them, but Bianca wasn't so certain. They were clubs run by the Ks, but they let humans come inside. The only humans who tended to go in were xenophiles, or K obsessed humans, which was why the clubs were called X-clubs. And once a human went inside, the odds of him or her ending up in a K's bed were high. Bianca knew why.

As the president's daughter, she had been educated about the Krinar more than just about anyone in the general public. She knew only too well which rumors were true and which weren't. The worst details about the Krinar, well, those were the ones that were mostly true.

The Krinar drank human blood. Not often, but they did it when having sex. Apparently it gave them some kind of pleasure high, and humans were similarly affected, like being given ecstasy that enhanced their sexual arousal beyond imagining. That wasn't something Bianca wanted to think about. The Ks were basically space vampires—not that she'd ever say that to their faces.

"Mandy said that her friend Lucy was sore for *days*." Claudia pointed discreetly below her waist.

"Seriously?"

"She didn't say *where*, though," Claudia giggled.

Bianca wished she wasn't fascinated, but she was. She was still a virgin, thanks to her agents. Any man who got too handsy with her was escorted home by her assigned Secret Service watchdogs. Daddy's orders.

"Oh yeah. She says she doesn't really remember much about what happened after one bit her, just that she was in some crazy kind of orgy."

"*Orgy?* Come on, Claudia, be serious." Bianca laughed. Orgies? Was she kidding?

"I *am* serious." Claudia frowned. "She slept with three guys, at least she thinks it was three. They were in some basement, and the furniture was floating."

Bianca snorted. Sadly, there wasn't an extra pillow on her bed to throw at her roommate. She was totally pulling her leg.

"Orgies and floating furniture? Why don't we just go back to sleep? We have two weeks until finals, and we should focus on that, not Krinar X-clubs and floating furniture."

Claudia huffed and turned off the light. Bianca settled back in her bed, pulled the covers up to her chin, and closed her eyes. But tonight she knew she would get little sleep, because Soren was there, a seductive, threatening shadow in the back of her mind. She stated known facts in her head to calm down.

Ks can't read minds. Truth.

Ks can't watch you sleep in your bed. Truth.

But they could see you in your dorm room if they decided to put cameras in here. Scary truth.

Soren doesn't know where you are, and he doesn't care. You're just the human president's brat he met once five years ago. Truth? She hoped so.

She drifted into a light, restless sleep and wondered why she couldn't shake the sense that someone was indeed watching her.

————

SOREN FROWNED AT THE HOLOGRAM OF THE HUMAN woman's dorm room, watching her toss and turn over the next three hours. He hadn't tapped into this feed in nearly four years, not since he'd assured himself that her college accommodations were suitable. She was the daughter of a great leader whom he respected, after all. It was only natural to check on her. For security. The anti-K rebels had been known to target pro-Krinar leaders and their families. The president wasn't exactly pro-Krinar, but he was supportive of peaceful relations and cooperation between their species.

Soren stared at the hologram of Bianca, and his frown deepened. Why she held such a curiosity for him, he didn't know. Perhaps because he knew she was curious about him, frightened by him too. After eight thousand long years of life, nothing much surprised or intrigued him these days. But she did. And it wasn't simply because she had grown up from a young human girl to an enchanting woman. Five years made quite a difference. He hadn't looked at her at sixteen the way he looked at her now. Now she was a grown woman.

Her long blonde hair was so unlike the dark shades of brown of his own people, and her eyes were almost a jade-like green with a hint of hazel. This was not an eye color one would see on his planet, Krina. They all had brown eyes, which sometimes warmed to gold whenever they experienced strong emotions.

Bianca Wells. He pulled up her course schedule on the Princeton servers to review the details. Her classes were all biology or zoology related. She would be obtaining her degree in a few weeks. If he understood the college servers' information correctly, she wished to become a marine biologist.

Interesting.

He leaned back in his chair, thinking. Earth had developed differently than Krina. His home world had but one giant land mass surrounded by a vast ocean. It was too dangerous to live closer than twenty miles from the shore because the strong tides were comparable to tsunamis on Earth. But here on the little blue planet with its separate continents and its many seas, they had the safety to explore it, to plumb its depths and swim alongside its creatures.

What would Bianca think if he showed her Krina

and the frightening dark pull of its dangerous waters? But he couldn't, wouldn't. He had to keep his distance. The last thing he needed was to find himself in charge of a charl, or what his people called a human companion. While the idea teased him with arousal he hadn't felt in years, he could not take the US president's daughter as his human pleasure companion. It would be seen as an act of war by President Wells, a violation of the Coexistence Treaty, and it would give the anti-Ks all the more reason to redouble their efforts to oust the Krinar from the planet, no matter that the Krinar were here to help them, to keep them from foolishly destroying their gift of a healthy planet and the young sun in their solar system. His people on Krina were on borrowed time. Their own sun in their system was dying, which had driven them to desperation, but fortunately this move to Earth had been eons in the making.

Soren turned off the screen, removing the temptation of Bianca from his mind for now.

"Soren?" Arus's voice came through the tablet on his desk. He waved a hand, activating the small implant in his palm that was connected with his mind. He could turn things on and off as well as perform other tasks in his home with thought alone.

Arus's face appeared on the screen.

"Arus, what may I help you with?" he asked the Krinar Council member.

"Two of our scientists have been accepted by several universities to start teaching Krinar history and basic science. I have a list of universities I would like them to visit. I'd like you to introduce our two teachers to the first university they will be teaching at this fall. Is this acceptable for you?"

"Of course." Soren didn't ask Arus why he wanted Soren to essentially babysit a couple of scientists, assuming Arus must have his reasons.

"Thank you. I've sent you the list of universities and the personnel files of our team members who will be meeting with you. They will arrive tomorrow morning."

"Very good," Soren replied. He was about to sever the connection when Arus spoke again. "I understand President Wells's daughter is attending one of the schools. Princeton. I believe you should request her to accompany you on the tour. It will provide good publicity if the campus sees Bianca Wells walking around with our people."

Soren cleared his throat, his blood humming with forbidden desire. "Are you sure?" He had just promised himself that he would leave Bianca alone, and now Arus was serving the delicious little woman to him on a platter. It would be impossible not to have a small taste of the pleasure she would give any male who took her to bed. He'd gone too long without a companion, had even gone too long without sharing his bed. He and his people had no sexual taboos the way humans did. They viewed sex as a thing to be shared and enjoyed, which made his relative celibacy rare. One did not need to have a partner or be in a lasting relationship to indulge. In the last five years, Soren's hungers and desires had been dormant. Seeing her tonight had brought his hard-edged arousal back to the surface.

"I'm certain. Bring Wells's daughter," Arus confirmed. Then his face vanished as he severed the connection.

Soren closed his eyes, drawing in a deep breath. It would take everything in him not to take Bianca tomorrow, *take* her and taste her. He entertained the thought of contacting an old female friend, someone to come and satisfy his urges, but that would not take the edge off the hunger that had stirred to life after seeing Bianca in bed tonight. He remembered how she had turned and kicked off her covers, revealing sleek, curvy legs and a bottom he wanted to sink his teeth into. And then there was the delicious curve of her neck and the slopes of her breasts beneath the loose cotton T-shirt she wore. What he wouldn't give to strip her bare and fuck the life out of her until her throat was raw from screaming in pleasure.

In eight thousand years, he'd never known a temptation like Bianca Wells.

CHAPTER 2

"That's weird..." Bianca stared at the inbox of her school email on her phone before putting on her short black ankle boots and pulling her jeans down over them.

Claudia lounged on her bed, a fat biochemistry book open in front of her and a fleet of slender Post-it notes scattered like brightly colored flower petals around her. "What's weird?"

"The university president just emailed me. He has some special guests coming on campus today. He wants me to join them on a tour."

"You *are* the president's daughter. I'm surprised Ackerman even kept his promise not to trot you out like a prized pony this long." Claudia highlighted something in her book, still not looking up.

"I know. Mr. Ackerman has been pretty low-key up

till now." She remembered her interview day, when the only question she'd had for him had been whether she would be able to feel like a normal college kid and not have her life on display to entertain big donors and that sort of thing. He had promised her that he would let her have a quiet, completely normal experience.

"Maybe since I'm only a few weeks away from graduating, he felt he could break his promise."

Claudia made a noise as though she was listening, but Bianca knew better. Claudia was deep into prepping for her biochemistry finals and couldn't afford any distractions. Bianca left her roommate alone and met her Secret Service agents, Mike and Scott, as she left her dorm room.

They'd been with her for the last four years, and were more like overprotective brothers than armed agents. They wore dark sunglasses and had the telltale little radios plugged in their ears.

Mike put his hand to his mouth, whispering as he communicated with another team off campus. "Hummingbird on the move." And then they were off, like a three-part machine, moving in tandem across campus. The agents didn't wear suits—they wore street clothes to keep attention to a minimum—but it was hard not to notice the two grim-faced men trailing close behind her.

When she was sixteen, she had hated the agents following her everywhere, but now she had grown used to them. They really weren't that bad, and they didn't completely destroy her social life. In recent years they'd eased up on her detail, probably because the threat to her life had decreased after K-Day. When the Krinar invaded, politics had changed on the global scale. The Ks were the *real* threat, and the rebellious factions of humans across the globe had become more united against them.

"Slight change in plans, guys," she told the agents as she steered away from the student union and headed toward the administrative building.

Scott frowned. "Oh?" He didn't like change because it could put her in danger if he couldn't clear a room or a setting before she arrived there safely.

"Mr. Ackerman wants me to join him on some tour around campus. He must have some heavy donors he wants to impress."

"He should've cleared that with the security detail last night" Mike began. Bianca put a hand on his arm and sighed.

"It's not a big deal, okay?" She trotted up the steps to the administration building and went inside.

Mr. Ackerman's office was on the first floor in a corner suite. Bianca smiled at his receptionist while she called the president on the phone. She listened to whatever he said and then nodded eagerly.

"Just have a seat, Ms. Wells. They'll be right out."

Bianca sat down, and the two agents hovered

nearby, one at the door and the other in the hallway. She summoned a polite smile as the door opened and President Ackerman stepped out of his office, but her smile faltered as she noticed who was behind him. Two Krinar, one a svelte female and the other an attractive, muscled male. Then her heart stopped as she caught sight of another Krinar male leaving the office.

Ambassador Soren is here. She felt dizzy with a sudden spell of vertigo.

"Ms. Wells, such a delight to have you accompanying us today..." Ackerman continued speaking, but she could barely understand him. Her head was buzzing as she drank in the sight of the man who'd starred in far too many of her dreams *and* nightmares. He wore a fitted light-gray pair of trousers and a black sweater that molded to his body enough to indicate his muscled physique. Other than his clothes, he hadn't changed one bit since she'd last seen him. The Krinar didn't age, she knew that, but she didn't know how that was possible. But he was an alien, and there was much humans didn't know about the Krinar. They kept their science and technology incredibly secret.

Soren was the creature of her nightmares, but he was also the only man she'd ever had sexual fantasies about, intense ones—sometimes dark ones that made her wake shivering and hungry for things that filled her with shame. Yet she couldn't deny the raw passion that thoughts of him could incite in her. It made it hard to take other men seriously when they asked her out because the only man she could think about was him.

It was messed up, but it was the truth. And it was something she wanted to bury out of sight. But that wouldn't be possible today. Not with the simmering heat coming from Soren as he looked into her eyes.

"Ms. Wells?" Ackerman's voice broke through the chaos of her thoughts.

She blushed. "Sorry, President Ackerman."

"This is Jaks." He nodded toward the male K, who smiled pleasantly at her. "And this is Driana." The female's smile was also warm and genuine. "You are familiar with Ambassador Soren, I believe?"

All she could manage was a nod.

"Good. Well, Jaks and Driana are going to start lectures this fall at Princeton. Ambassador Soren knew you attended here and believed it might be beneficial to share your experiences with our new professors."

Knowing this was not a time she could turn and escape, she had to grin and bear the situation as best she could. She stepped up to Driana, and Driana trailed the backs of her knuckles down Bianca's left cheek in greeting. Bianca returned it. "It's nice to meet you." She had learned the Krinar greeting years ago. She stepped toward Jaks to do the same, but he gave a slight shake of his head when Soren made a low sound that sounded suspiciously like a growl. Was he honest to God growling? Jaks didn't look Soren's way, but his smile was still warm as he nodded in greeting instead.

Soren didn't approach her, and for that she was thankful. If he had touched her, she honestly didn't know what she would have done. He continued to watch her, his eyes giving her body an invisible caress that made her break out in goosebumps.

Ackerman cleared his throat. "Well...er...shall we start the tour?"

For the next two hours, she and Ackerman worked together to present the prestigious history of Princeton and answer any questions the Ks had about the university and college life. Jaks and Driana were polite and clearly interested in the human college experience. Soren remained silent except when the other Ks asked him something. The entire time, his focus remained fixed on her. Her blood heated beneath her skin each time she glanced his way and found him intensely watching her. This was so different from five years ago. She'd been dismissed so quickly then, but now she had caught his attention and couldn't shake it.

"You enjoy living in these dormitories?" Jaks inquired as they paused before one of the many housing structures on campus. "They seem...small."

"College students enjoy being around people our own age. Sometimes it can be like a party. I like the quiet more, but my roommate, Claudia, is fun."

Driana lifted her head back as she studied the tall

red brick dorm. "In our settlements, we prefer a little more space. We spread out rather than live on top of one another." Her observation was not made with condescension but rather with curiosity.

Soren spoke up. "We are *highly* territorial, aren't we, Jaks?"

Bianca's gaze darted between the two handsome men, and she thought she saw amusement in Jaks's eyes before he replied.

"Certainly some more than others."

President Ackerman watched the exchange, clearly puzzled, before he clapped his hands together. "Right, well, the library is next."

They headed to Princeton's Firestone Library, and the Ks murmured among themselves in appreciation at the modern blend of stone and glass. Giant circular chandeliers that Claudia called "the glowing dough-nuts" illuminated one of the main study areas.

"Why don't I show you our oldest archives? We have some impressive first editions of some of the greatest human literature." Ackerman led the way. Bianca knew they would come back eventually to leave, so she remained by the entryway closest to the stacks. She hoped it would give her a moment to avoid Soren while he joined them in the archives portion of the library. Only he didn't move around her, didn't go with the other Ks. He stayed right there behind her, the heat of his body so close she could feel it. Mike and

Scott shifted restlessly from their positions fifteen feet away, but she didn't call for help.

"It has been a long time, Bianca," Soren said, his voice low and soft, dangerously sweet. Bianca knew better than to trust that voice, no matter how much she had fantasized about it over the years, albeit in a very different context.

"It has." She moved deeper into the stacks, not wanting any students to see them talking. Her security detail kept a discreet distance.

"And you have been well?" he asked, still in that soft, dangerous tone that made her shiver, and her thighs tightened. "When I meet with your father, he rarely speaks of you. He focuses only on business."

"Yes, he's good that way," she replied. "I don't like him to talk about me." *Especially to you,* she thought.

Soren leaned against the stacks to her left, blocking her exit. She looked up at him. She was not short by any means at five feet six inches, but Soren was six foot seven and made her feel tiny. A shiver rippled through her, and it didn't escape his notice.

"Are you cold?" He removed a device from his pocket, no bigger than a computer mouse, and before she could stop him, he pressed a button. A beam of light shot into the air, and she was shocked to see a thin pale-gray jacket materialize in front of her. He slipped the device back into his pocket and retrieved the jacket, which still hung suspended in the air, then slipped her arms into it. She knew from her father's meetings that what he used was called a fabricator. The Ks had such advanced technology that they could produce almost anything they desired using such a tiny device.

His hands lingered a moment longer on her shoulders than was appropriate for two strangers. But they weren't strangers, were they? And how often had she dreamed about him? Fantasized about those hands on her body, stroking, caressing, teasing her? Too many times. Her screams of fear all too often had turned to screams of pleasure as she'd awakened in the dark, her body dewed with sweat and her panties wet with her desire.

It always filled her with shame, to be turned on by an alien, especially the one who'd put her father in his place like a trained dog and had taken over the running of Earth so smoothly. But there was no denying the power Soren had over her in the realm of dreams. How he would trap her beneath him on a bed, pumping into her over and over, his teeth sinking into her neck, and how she'd obliterate into a thousand pieces as a primal, overwhelming climax rocked her to her core.

The way he was looking at her now, as though he could read her thoughts, made his eyes flash gold and his lips part slightly. His warm breath fanned her face, and she trembled at the heat building between them. It was as though they were at the heart of a dying star, spirals of light spinning outward from them. She'd seen that once on a science show, and she'd never forgotten the beautiful image. Now she felt as if she were living that within that moment.

He slowly released her but didn't move away.

"You...you didn't need to do that." She wished she could shrug off the clothing made by his alien technology. But the jacket fit perfectly. Of course it did. Everything the Ks did was perfect, right down to controlling the lives of humans. She was all too aware of the fact that right now he could do anything to her that he liked, and it wouldn't be against any of the laws because Ks were above human laws. *They* were in charge.

"There's far more pleasure in doing what one *wants* than what one *needs*, don't you agree?" He brushed his knuckles down her cheek in greeting, but unlike with Driana, it was not an innocent gesture. His touch left a burning sensation on her skin that made her head spin, and he leaned down until their faces were a few inches apart. His brown eyes swirled into honey gold again, and his dark, masculine scent surrounded her. He repeated the light caress to her other cheek, and she couldn't stop herself from reacting. When she leaned into that touch, he stopped breathing for a few seconds, and so did she.

Her eyes locked with his, and her desire for him,

the thing she hated most about herself, seemed too strong to fight.

"You tempt me, Bianca. Tempt me to break my own rules."

She stared at his full lips now, fascinated by the sensual curve of them as he smiled. "What rules?"

"I didn't want to get involved with a human, especially not one as politically important as you, but..." He cupped her chin, his face moving even closer. "But it seems I can't deny myself."

It was the only warning she had before his lips stole hers. The kiss exploded with the force of a bursting supernova. His lips nibbled at hers, his tongue winning entrance to her mouth. He tasted so good, unexpectedly sweet, which Bianca puzzled over as she gripped his sweater to draw him closer. The thrill of his kiss startled her so much that she didn't resist, didn't push away. No, her treacherous body burrowed closer to his, and his low, purring approval flushed her body from head to toe with spirals of wild heat. Her pulse pounded as he moved his head lower to her throat. He flicked his tongue against her skin before dragging the tips of his sharp teeth along her neck, causing a light rasping sensation.

A moan so loud it mortified her escaped her lips as she grew wet. His teeth moved to the crook between her neck and shoulder, sinking slightly deeper. Was he going to bite her?

"Please..." Bianca breathed a plea, but she honestly wasn't sure if she was asking him to stop or to keep going.

"Please what, *lilana*?" He gathered her into his arms, and the scent of him washing over her made her delightfully dizzy.

"What does that mean? *Lilana?*"

Soren nuzzled her neck, his lips moving in soft whispers over her skin. "It means *precious one* in my tongue."

Precious one? How could she be precious to him? He was a K, and she was human. She knew how he viewed her people. His words from five years ago to her father still echoed in her head.

"You have been poor custodians of such a precious planet. You have ruined it. We are here to fix what we can, and you will be thankful for the intervention."

The memory was a cold slap to her face. She flattened her palms on his chest and shoved. Hard. The muscled mass of Soren's tall form didn't budge. Tears of rage and shame pricked her eyes. She hated being weak, and only Soren made her feel like this. She was helpless around him, a toy, nothing of consequence.

He pulled back and stared down at her, concern darkening his eyes. His russet hair, a rare color among the Krinar, fell into his eyes. Had he been any other man, she would have reached up to brush it away from his beautiful, predatory eyes. But she didn't dare. His pull was undeniable, and to touch him would be to risk everything.

"Ms. Wells, are you all right?" Scott asked.

The agent's voice drew her eyes away from Soren. Scott and Mike hovered like overprotective mother hens. A fresh wave of mortification rolled through her. She had been caught making out in the stacks like some college freshman, with a damned Krinar! And her agents, two men she trusted with her life, were frowning in disapproval, their faces pale, and each looked ready to draw his weapon.

"I...I'm fine." She gave the agents a grateful smile, but they all knew that if they dared to attack or restrain Soren, he was capable of ripping them to pieces. Krinar were incredibly fast and strong.

Everyone had seen the footage of a Middle Eastern terrorist cell that had tried to fight off just one Krinar male. The male had been hit by a sniper's bullet during a surprise attack, and that had only pissed him off. He'd rushed their position and torn them to pieces with his bare hands in a blood-fueled rage. If Soren wanted her, Mike and Scott would die trying to protect her from him, but they *would* die. She wouldn't let that happen. She would surrender to him if she had to in order to protect those two good men.

"Will the tour be over soon?" Soren asked, ignoring the agents.

"I think so. Ackerman doesn't have much else to show them."

Soren's lips curved in the ghost of a smile. "Good. When it is over, you and I shall talk." He stepped away and exited the stacks to wait in the entryway for his fellow Ks to return.

Bianca ran her hands through her hair and struggled to grip the frayed ends of her self-control. Soren wanted her. She had felt the press of his shaft against her belly as he'd kissed her, and the blazing heat in his promise of what he wished to do with her. What was she going to do? There was no escaping this.

"Bianca," Mike whispered softly, but even he knew that Soren could probably still hear them. "You sure you're okay? We can take you away, call your father"

"No!" she hissed. If they called him, he would be furious, and that would risk the peaceful relationship between Earth and Krina. The Coexistence Treaty was in place, but that didn't mean it couldn't be broken if she was foolish enough to resist. Lives could be lost, and they could be enslaved more than they were now. At least right now the human race could tolerate their situation. The Ks ran the show, but they let human lives go on mostly unaffected. But all of that could change if she dared to resist whatever Soren wanted from her.

"You sure?" Scott pressed. "He wasn't following protocol. It should be reported."

"No. You know as well as I do what that could lead to. If he comes back to my dorm, stay outside. *Please.*" She reached out to touch both men on the shoulders, but the heavy sound of a distant growl made her hands freeze inches from their skin. She drew a slow breath.

Krinar males are possessive. Truth.

Krinar males will not let another man touch what they believe is theirs. Truth.

But she wasn't his. She was her own person, and she would never belong to anyone the way Soren seemed to want her to belong to him.

She rejoined Soren in the foyer of the library just as Ackerman and the two Krinar professors returned.

"There is something so amazing about your books," Driana said with a soft, appreciative smile. "I feel sorrow for the trees destroyed, yet the books themselves with their stories and knowledge pay tribute to the plants that bore them."

Jaks nodded sagely. "Well said."

Bianca watched the two alien professors, still surprised by their genuine warmth and friendliness. She had only ever met Krinar like Soren before, the kind who dealt with politics and those who had conquered the world. It was easy to imagine the Krinar as only bloodthirsty warriors, not like these inquisitive and kind Krinar. They had shown only respect and curiosity for her world and the lives of the college students. There had been no condescension, no looking down their noses at their primitive human ways.

"Well." Ackerman smiled at the group. "I think we've seen enough today. You're welcome back anytime before August, of course. I'll have your offices prepared in the buildings belonging to your respective fields of study, medicine, and Krinar and human biology."

"Biology?" Bianca couldn't resist piping up. "Which one of you is teaching that?"

Driana grinned. "I am. Is that an interest of yours?"

"Yes!" Bianca said, forgetting for a moment about Soren, who had come up close behind her.

"I'm studying marine biology. I would love to speak with you about Krinar marine life, if you are familiar with it. I won't be here this fall since I'm graduating, so I'll miss your class. Can I meet with you instead?"

Driana's gaze drifted above Bianca's head to something behind her, the female K's expression searching for a moment before she smiled again and nodded.

"Soon. Very soon, little one," Driana promised. She held out her hand and caressed Bianca's face, and Bianca, thrilled at the prospect of talking to a Krinar biologist, returned the greeting with a smile. Her heart was bursting with excitement as she watched the university president escort Jaks and Driana away.

Then only she and Soren were left, along with her security detail.

"Show me to your dorm, Bianca." Soren's

command was gentle, but it was still an order. He reached out to catch one of her hands as he said this, his warm palm covering hers completely. She knew he wouldn't let her go if she tried to pull away. Domination shone in his gaze, even if it was gentled by a soft half smile. She bristled at his command, but she didn't say anything. She headed off to her room, her hand still entwined with his.

She was doomed. There was no preventing whatever was to come.

WANT TO SEE HOW BIANCA HANDLES SEXY AMBASSADOR Soren? Get the book HERE!

OTHER TITLES BY EMMA CASTLE

EMMA CASTLE
Dark and Edgy Romance

Unlikely Heroes
*can be read as standalones
Midnight with the Devil - Book 1
A Wilderness Within - Book 2

Sci-Fi Romance - The Krinar World
The Krinar Eclipse by Lauren Smith
The Krinar Code by Emma Castle

ABOUT THE AUTHOR

Emma Castle has always loved reading but didn't know she loved romance until she was enduring the trials of law school. She discovered the dark and sexy world of romance novels and since then has never looked back! She loves writing about sexy, alpha male heroes who know just how to seduce women even if they are a bit naughty about it. When Emma's not writing, she may be obsessing over her favorite show Supernatural where she's a total Team Dean Winchester kind of girl!

If you wish to be added to Emma's new release newsletter feel free to contact Emma using the Sign up link on her website at www.emmacastlebooks.com or email her at emma@emmacastlebooks.com!

facebook.com/Emmacastlebooks

twitter.com/emmacastlebooks

instagram.com/Emmacastlebooks

bookbub.com/authors/emma-castle